DOVER · THRIFT · EDITIONS

Everyman

and
Other Miracle and
Morality Plays

ANONYMOUS

DOVER PUBLICATIONS, INC.
New York

DOVER THRIFT EDITIONS

GENERAL EDITOR: STANLEY APPELBAUM
EDITOR OF THIS VOLUME: CANDACE WARD

Copyright

Performance

This Dover Thrift Edition may be used in its entirety, in adaptation or in any other way for theatrical productions, professional and amateur, in the United States, without fee, permission or acknowledgment. (This may not apply outside of the United States, as copyright conditions may vary.)

Bibliographical Note

This Dover edition, first published in 1995, is a new collection of plays reprinted from the following sources: *Everyman and Other Old Religious Plays*, edited by Ernest Rhys (London: J.M. Dent & Sons Ltd., Everyman's Library, 1909; *Noah's Flood* [under the title *The Deluge*] and *Everyman*); *The Second Shepherds' Play, Everyman and Other Early Plays*, translated by Clarence Griffin Child (Boston: Houghton Mifflin Company, The Riverside Press, 1910; *The Second Shepherds' Play*); *Early English Dramatists: Six Anonymous Plays* (London: Early English Drama Society, 1905; *Hickscorner*). Explanatory footnotes and an introductory Note have been prepared specially for this edition.

Library of Congress Cataloging-in-Publication Data

Everyman, and other miracle and morality plays / Anonymous.
    p.   cm. — (Dover thrift editions)
    Contents: Noah's flood — The second shepherds' play — Everyman — Hickscorner.
    ISBN 0-486-28726-2 (pbk.)
    1. Mysteries and miracle-plays, English.   2. Christian drama, English (Middle)
3. Christian ethics—Drama.   4. English drama—To 1500.   5. Moralities,
English.   I. Series.
PR1260.E92   1995
822'.051608—dc20   95-37086
                                                                         CIP

Manufactured in the United States of America
Dover Publications, Inc., 31 East 2nd Street, Mineola, N.Y. 11501

Note

Rooted in the liturgy of the early Western Church, the drama of the Middle Ages provided a bridge between the ecclesiastical and secular elements of medieval life. "Miracle" and "morality" plays were performed on holidays and at festivals by guild craftsmen or professional actors, hired by towns and villages for the occasion. The morality plays, such as *Everyman* (after 1485) and *Hickscorner* (ca. 1497–1512), were allegorical dramas featuring personifications of Mankind and various helps (Goodwill, Mercy, Perseverance, etc.) or hindrances (Vice, Imagination, Goods, etc.) he encountered on the road to salvation. The "miracle" (or "mystery") plays dramatized scriptural events, as in *The Second Shepherds' Play* and *Noah's Flood*. The miracle plays were written in cycles, groups or series of plays, each about a specific biblical event. The cycles typically began with the Creation and proceeded through biblical history. Only four such cycles have survived intact: the York cycle (early 14th century), the Towneley, or Wakefield, cycle (mid-14th century–early 15th century), the Chester cycle (14th century) and the Coventry cycle (15th century). *The Second Shepherds' Play*, so called because it is the second of two plays about the Nativity, is part of the Towneley cycle and *Noah's Flood* is part of the Chester cycle.

Contents

NOAH'S FLOOD

(*From the Chester cycle*)

CHARACTERS

GOD	NOAH'S WIFE
NOAH	SHEM'S WIFE
SHEM	HAM'S WIFE
HAM	JAPHET'S WIFE
JAPHET	

God.   I, God, that all the world have wrought
    Heaven and Earth, and all of nought,
    I see my people, in deed and thought,
    Are foully set in sin.
      My ghost shall not lodge in any man
    That through fleshly liking is my fone,[1]
    But till six score years be gone
    To look if they will blynne.[2]
      Man that I made I will destroy,
    Beast, worm, and fowl to fly,
    For on earth they me annoy,
    The folk that is thereon.
      For it harms me so hurtfully
    The malice now that can multiply,
    That sore it grieveth me inwardly,
    That ever I made man.
      Therefore Noah, my servant free,

---

1. *fone*] foe.
2. *blynne*] stop, cease.

That righteous man art, as I see,
A ship soon thou shalt make thee,
Of trees dry and light.
    Little chambers therein thou make
And binding slich[3] also thou take
Within and out, thou not slake[4]
To annoint it through all thy might.
    Three hundred cubits it shall be long,
And so of breadth to make it strong,
Of height so, then must thou fonge,[5]
Thus measure it about.
    One window work though thy might;
One cubit of length and breadth make it,
Upon the side a door shall fit
For to come in and out.
    Eating-places thou make also,
Three roofed chambers, one or two:
For with water I think to stow[6]
Man that I can make.
    Destroyed all the world shall be,
Save thou, thy wife, and sons three,
And all their wives, also, with thee,
Shall saved be for thy sake.

Noah.   Ah, Lord! I thank thee, loud and still,
That to me art in such will,
And spares me and my house to spill
As now I soothly find.
    Thy bidding, Lord, I shall fulfil,
And never more thee grieve nor grill[7]
That such grace has sent me till
Among all mankind.
    Have done you men and women all;
Help, for aught that may befall,
To work this ship, chamber, and hall,
As God hath bidden us do.

Shem.   Father, I am already bowne,[8]
An axe I have, by my crown!

---

3. *slich*] slime or pitch (to make watertight).
4. *slake*] abate, subside.
5. *fonge*] take.
6. *stow*] hinder, stop.
7. *grill*] vex.
8. *bowne*] prepared.

As sharp as any in all this town
For to go thereto.
Ham.   I have a hatchet, wonder keen,
To bite well, as may be seen,
A better ground one, as I ween,[9]
Is not in all this town.
Japhet.   And I can well make a pin,
And with this hammer knock it in;
Go and work without more din;
And I am ready bowne.
Noah's Wife.   And we shall bring timber too,
For women nothing else to do
Women be weak to undergo
Any great travail.
Shem's Wife.   Here is a good hackstock;[10]
On this you must hew and knock:
Shall none be idle in this flock,
Nor now may no man fail.
Ham's Wife.   And I will go to gather slich,
The ship for to clean and pitch;
Anointed it must be, every stitch,
Board, tree, and pin.
Japhet's Wife.   And I will gather chips here
To make a fire for you, in fear,
And for to dight[11] your dinner,
Against[12] you come in.

[Here they make signs as though they were working with divers instruments.]

Noah.   Now in the name of God I will begin,
To make the ship that we shall in,
That we be ready for to swim,
At the coming of the flood.
These boards I join together,
To keep us safe from the weather
That we may roam both hither and thither
And safe be from this flood.
Of this tree will I have the mast,

9. *ween*] imagine.
10. *hackstock*] building wood(?).
11. *dight*] prepare.
12. *Against*] In preparation for the time when . . .; before.

Tied with gables that will last
With a sail yard for each blast
And each thing in its kind.
    With topmast high and bowsprit,
With cords and ropes, I hold all fit
To sail forth at the next weete[13]
This ship is at an end.
Wife in this castle we shall be kept:
My children and thou I would in leaped!

Noah's Wife.   In faith, Noe, I had as lief thou had slept, for all thy
        frankishfare,[14]
    For I will not do after thy rede.[15]

Noah.   Good wife, do as I thee bid.

Noah's Wife.   By Christ not, or I see more need,
    Though thou stand all the day and rave.

Noah.   Lord, that women be crabbed aye!
    And never are meek, that I dare say.
    This is well seen of me to-day
    In witness of you each one.
        Good wife, let be all this beere[16]
    That thou makest in this place here,
    For they all ween[17] thou art master;
    And so thou art, by St. John!

God.   Noah, take thou thy company
    And in the ship hie[18] that you be,
    For none so righteous man to me
    Is now on earth living.
        Of clean beasts with thee thou take
    Seven and seven, or thou seake,[19]
    He and she make to make
    Quickly in that thou bring.
        Of beasts unclean two and two,
    Male and female, without more;
    Of clean fowls seven also,
    The he and she together.
        Of fowles unclean two, and no more;

---

13. *weete*] tide.
14. *frankishfare*] nonsense.
15. *rede*] advice, counsel.
16. *beere*] noise.
17. *ween*] imagine.
18. *hie*] hurry, hasten.
19. *seake*] seek.

Of beasts as I said before:
That shall be saved through my lore[20]
Against I send the weather.
        Of all meats that must be eaten
Into the ship look there be gotten,
For that no way may be forgotten
And do all this by deene.[21]
        To sustain man and beasts therein,
Aye, till the waters cease and blyn.[22]
This world is filled full of sin
And that is now well seen.
      Seven days be yet coming,
You shall have space them in to bring;
After that it is my liking
Mankind for to annoy.
        Forty days and forty nights,
Rain shall fall for their unrights;
And that I have made through my might,
Now think I to destroy.

Noah.   Lord, at your bidding I am bayne,[23]
Since none other grace will gain,
It will I fulfil fain,[24]
For gracious I thee find.
        A hundred winters and twenty
This ship making tarried have I:
If, through amendment, any mercy
Would fall unto mankind.
        Have done, you men and women all.
Hie you, lest this water fall,
That each beast were in his stall
And into ship brought.
        Of clean beasts seven shall be;
Of unclean two, this God bade me;
This flood is nigh, well may we see,
Therefore tarry you nought.

Shem.   Sir, here are lions, leopards in,
Horses, mares, oxen, and swine,

20. *lore*] knowledge.
21. *by deene*] immediately.
22. *blyn*] stop.
23. *bayne*] ready.
24. *fain*] gladly, with pleasure.

Goats, calves, sheep, and kine,[25]
Here sitten[26] may you see.
Ham.   Camels, asses, men may find;
Buck, doe, hart and hind,
And beasts of all manner kind.
Here be, as thinks me.
Japhet.   Take here cats and dogs too,
Otter, fox, fulmart[27] also;
Hares, hopping gaily, can ye
Have kail[28] here for to eat.
Noah's Wife.   And here are bears, wolves set,
Apes, owls, marmoset;
Weasels, squirrels, and ferret
Here they eat their meat.
Shem's Wife.   Yet more beasts are in this house!
Here cats come in full crowse,[29]
Here a rat and here a mouse;
They stand nigh together.
Ham's Wife.   And here are fowls less and more,
Herons, cranes and bittern;[30]
Swans, peacocks, have them before!
Meat for this weather.
Japhet's Wife.   Here are cocks, kites, crows,
Rooks, ravens, many rows;
Cuckoos, curlews, whoso knows,
Each one in his kind.
     And here are doves, ducks, drakes,
Redshanks, running through the lakes,
And each fowl that language makes
In this ship men may find.

[*In the stage direction the sons of Noah are enjoined to mention aloud the names of the animals which enter; a representation of which, painted on parchment, is to be carried by the actors.*]

Noah.   Wife, come in, why standest thou there?
Thou art ever forward, that I dare swear:

25. *kine*] cows.
26. *sitten*] settled.
27. *fulmart*] an arctic sea bird resembling the herring gull in size and color.
28. *kail*] kale; cabbage-type plant.
29. *crowse*] comfortable.
30. *bittern*] any member of a subfamily (*Botaurinae*) of herons.

Come on God's half,[31] time it were,
    For fear lest that we drown.
Noah's Wife.   Yea, sir, set up your sail
    And row forth with evil heale,[32]
    For, without any fail,
    I will not out of this town.
      But I have my gossips[33] every one,
    One foot further I will not go;
    They shall not drown, by St. John!
    If I may save their life.
      They loved me full well, by Christ!
    But thou wilt let them in thy chest,
    Else row forth, Noah, whither thou list,
    And get thee a new wife.
Noah.   Shem, some love thy mother, 'tis true;
    Forsooth, such another I do not know!
Shem.   Father, I shall set her in, I trow,
    Without any fail.
      Mother, my father after thee sends,
    And bids thee unto yonder ship wend,[34]
    Look up and see the wind,
    For we be ready to sail.
Noah's Wife.   Son, go again to him and say
    I will not come therein to-day!
Noah.   Come in, wife, in twenty devils' way,
    Or else stand without.
Ham.   Shall we all fetch her in?
Noah.   Yea, sons, in Christ's blessing and mine,
    I would you hied you betime,
    For of this flood I am in doubt.
Japhet.   Mother, we pray you altogether,
    For we are here, your children;
    Come into the ship for fear of the weather,
    For his love that you bought!
Noah's Wife.   That I will not for your call,
    But if I have my gossips all.
Gossip.   The flood comes in full fleeting fast,
    On every side it broadens in haste;

31. *half*] behalf.
32. *heale*] welfare, well-being.
33. *gossips*] friends, companions.
34. *wend*] go.

For fear of drowning I am aghast:
Good gossip, let me come in!
    Or let us drink ere we depart,
For oftentimes we have done so;
For at a time thou drinkst a quart,
And so will I ere that I go.
Shem.   In faith, mother, yet you shall,
    Whether you will or not!   [*She goes.*]
Noah.   Welcome, wife, into this boat!
Noah's Wife.   And have them that for thy note!35

[*Et dat alapam victa.*]36

Noah.   Aha! marry, this is hot!
    It is good to be still.
    My children! methinks this boat removes!37
    Our tarrying here hugely me grieves!
    Over the land the water spreads!
    God do as he will!
        Ah, great God, thou art so good!
    Now all this world is in a flood
    As I see well in sight.
        This window will I close anon,
    And into my chamber will I gone
    Till this water, so great one,
    Be slakèd through thy might.

[*Noah, according to stage directions, is now to shut the windows of the ark and retire for a short time. He is then to chant the psalm, Salva me, Domine! and afterwards to open them and look out.*]

    Now forty days are fully gone.
    Send a raven I will anon;
    If aught were earth, tree, or stone,
    Be dry in any place.
        And if this fowl come not again
    It is a sign, sooth to say,
    That dry it is on hill or plain,
    And God hath done some grace.

[*A raven is now despatched.*]

35. *note*] business, occupation.
36. *Et dat alapam victa.*] "And being conquered she deals a slap."
37. *removes*] shifts, changes position.

Ah, Lord! wherever this raven lie,
Somewhere is dry well I see;
But yet a dove, by my lewtye[38]
After I will send.
Thou wilt turn again to me
For of all fowls that may fly
Thou art most meek and hend.[39]

[*The stage direction enjoins here that another dove shall be ready with an olive branch in its mouth, which is to be dropped by means of a cord into Noah's hand.*]

Ah Lord! blessed be thou aye,
That me hast comforted thus to-day!
By this sight, I may well say
This flood begins to cease.
My sweet dove to me brought has
A branch of olive from some place;
This betokeneth God has done us some grace,
And is a sign of peace.
Ah, Lord! honoured must thou be!
All earth dries now I see;
But yet, till thou command me,
Hence will I not hie.
All this water is away,
Therefore as soon as I may
Sacrifice I shall do in faye[40]
To thee devoutly.

God.   Noah, take thy wife anon,
And thy children every one,
Out of the ship thou shalt gone,
And they all with thee.
Beasts and all that can flie,
Out anon they shall hie,
On earth to grow and multiply:
I will that it be so.

Noah.   Lord, I thank thee, through thy might,
Thy bidding shall be done in hight,[41]
And, as fast as I may dight

38. *lewtye*] fidelity.
39. *hend*] kind.
40. *faye*] faith.
41. *hight*] haste.

I will do thee honour.
  And to thee offer sacrifice,
Therefore comes in all wise,
For of these beasts that be his
Offer I will this stower.[42]

[*Then leaving the ark with his whole family, he shall take the animals and birds, make an offering of them, and set out on his way.*]

  Lord God, in majesty,
That such grace has granted me,
When all was borne safe to be,
Therefore now I am boune.[43]
  My wife, my children, my company,
With sacrifice to honour thee,
With beasts, fowls, as thou may see,
I offer here right soon.

God. Noah, to me thou art full able,
And thy sacrifice acceptable,
For I have found thee true and stable,
On thee now must I myn.[44]
Curse earth will I no more
That man's sin it grieves sore,
For of youth man full of yore
Has been inclined to sin.
  You shall now grow and multiply
And earth you edify,
Each beast and fowl that may flie
Shall be afraid for you.
  And fish in sea that may flitt
Shall sustain you — I you behite[45]
To eat of them you not lett[46]
That clean be you may know.
  There as you have eaten before
Grasses and roots, since you were born,
Of clean beasts, less and more,
I give you leave to eat.
  Save blood and fish both in fear
Of wrong dead carrion that is here,

42. *stower*] steer.
43. *boune*] ready.
44. *On . . . myn.*] I must have you in mind (myn) now.
45. *behite*] promise.
46. *lett*] cease.

Eat not of that in no manner,
For that aye you shall lett.[47]

    Manslaughter also you shall flee,
For that is not pleasant to me
That sheds blood, he or she
Ought where among mankind.

    That sheds blood, his blood shall be
And vengeance have, that men shall see;
Therefore now beware now all ye
You fall not in that sin.
And forward now with you I make
And all thy seed, for thy sake,
Of such vengeance for to slake,
For now I have my will.

    Here I promise thee a behest,[48]
That man, woman, fowl, nor beast
With water while the world shall last,
I will no more spill.

    My bow between you and me
In the firmament shall be,
By very tokens, that you may see
That such vengeance shall cease.

    That man, nor woman, shall never more
Be wasted by water, as is before,
But for sin that grieveth sore,
Therefore this vengeance was.

    Where clouds in the welkin[49]
That each bow shall be seen,
In token that my wrath or tene[50]
Should never this wroken[51] be.

    The string is turned toward you,
And toward me bent is the bow,
That such weather shall never show,
And this do I grant to thee.

    My blessing now I give thee here,
To thee Noah, my servant dear;
For vengeance shall no more appear;
And now farewell, my darling dear!

47. *lett*] here, leave (alone).
48. *behest*] covenant.
49. *welkin*] heaven, firmament.
50. *tene*] anger.
51. *wroken*] wreaked.

THE SECOND SHEPHERDS' PLAY

(From the Towneley cycle)

CHARACTERS

1ST SHEPHERD	GILL, MAK'S WIFE
2ND SHEPHERD	MARY
3RD SHEPHERD	THE CHILD CHRIST
MAK, *the Sheep-stealer*	AN ANGEL

[*The 1st Shepherd[1] enters.*]

1st Shepherd.   Lord, but this weather is cold, and I am ill wrapped!
　　Nigh dazed, were the truth told, so long have I napped;
　　My legs under me fold; my fingers are chapped —
　　With such like I don't hold, for I am all lapt
　　　　In sorrow.
　　In storms and tempest,
　　Now in the east, now in the west,
　　Woe is him has never rest
　　　　Midday nor morrow!

　　But we seely[2] shepherds that walk on the moor,
　　In faith we're nigh at hand to be put out of door.
　　No wonder, as it doth stand, if we be poor,
　　For the tilth[3] of our land lies fallow as the floor,
　　　　As ye ken.[4]

---

1. *1st Shepherd*] In some texts, the 1st, 2nd and 3rd Shepherds are given the names Coll, Gib and Daw.
2. *seely*] silly; blameless and to be pitied, "poor."
3. *tilth*] cultivated, arable land.
4. *ken*] know.

We're so burdened and banned,
Over-taxed and unmanned,
We're made tame to the hand
      Of these gentry men.

Thus they rob us of our rest, our Lady them harry!
These men bound to their lords' behest, they make the plough
    tarry,
What men say is for the best, we find the contrary, —
Thus are husbandmen oppressed, in point to miscarry,[5]
      In life,
Thus hold they us under
And from comfort sunder.
It were great wonder,
      If ever we should thrive.

For if a man may get an embroidered sleeve[6] or a brooch now-
    a-days,
Woe is him that may him grieve, or a word in answer says!
No blame may he receive, whatever pride he displays;
And yet may no man believe one word that he says,
      Not a letter.
His daily needs are gained
By boasts and bragging feigned,
And in all he's maintained
      By men that are greater.

Proud shall come a swain as a peacock may go,
He must borrow my wain,[7] my plough also,
Then I am full fain[8] to grant it ere he go.
Thus live we in pain, anger, and woe
      By night and day!
He must have it, if he choose,
Though I should it lose,
I were better hanged than refuse,
      Or once say him nay!

It does me good as I walk thus alone
Of this world for to talk and to make my moan.[9]

---

5. *in point to miscarry*] to the point of ruin.
6. *embroidered sleeve*] sign of authority.
7. *wain*] wagon.
8. *fain*] glad.
9. *moan*] complaint.

To my sheep will I stalk, and hearken anon,
There wait on a balk,[10] or sit on a stone.
          Full soon,
For I trow, pardie,[11]
True men if they be,
We shall have company,
          Ere it be noon.

[*The First Shepherd goes out (or to one side). The 2nd Shepherd enters.*]

2nd Shepherd.   Ben'cite[12] and Dominus! What may this mean?
Why fares the world thus! The like often we've seen!
Lord, but it is spiteful and grievous, this weather so keen!
And the frost so hideous — it waters mine een![13]
          That's no lie!
Now in dry, now in wet,
Now in snow, now in sleet,
When my shoes freeze to my feet,
          It's not all easy!

But so far as I ken, wherever I go,
We seely wedded men suffer mickle[14] woe,
We have sorrow once and again, it befalls oft so.
Seely Capel,[15] our hen, both to and fro
          She cackles,
But if she begins to croak,
To grumble or cluck,
Then woe be to our cock,
          For he is in the shackles![16]

These men that are wed have not all their will;
When they're full hard bestead,[17] they sigh mighty still;
God knows the life they are led is full hard and full ill,
Nor thereof in bower or bed may they speak their will,
          This tide.

---

10. *balk*] ridge or hillock.
11. *pardie*] par Dieu (by God).
12. *Ben'cite*] Shortened form of *benedicite* — "bless you!" — frequent in mediaeval use both
    as a salutation and exclamation.
13. *een*] eyes.
14. *mickle*] much.
15. *Capel*] slang for "wife."
16. *in the shackles*] in a tight place, under constraint to take what he gets.
17. *bestead*] beset.

My share I have found,
Know my lesson all round,
Woe is him that is bound,
      For he must it abide!

But now late in men's lives (such a marvel to me
That I think my heart rives[18] such wonders to see,
How that destiny drives that it should so be!)
Some men will have two wives and some men three
      In store.
Some are grieved that have any,
But I'll wager my penny
Woe is him that has many,
      For he feels sore!

But young men as to wooing, for God's sake that you bought,
Beware well of wedding, and hold well in thought,
"Had I known" is a thing that serves you nought.
Much silent sorrowing has a wedding home brought,
      And grief gives,
With many a sharp shower—
For thou mayest catch in an hour
What shall taste thee full sour
      As long as one lives!

For—if ever read I epistle!—I have one by my fire,
As sharp as a thistle, as rough as a briar,
She has brows like a bristle and a sour face by her;
If she had once wet her whistle, she might sing clearer and higher
      Her pater-noster;
She is as big as a whale,
She has a gallon of gall,—
By him that died for us all,
      I wish I had run till I had lost her!

1st Shepherd.   "God look over the row!"[19] like a deaf man ye stand.
2nd Shepherd.   Yea, sluggard, the devil thy maw[20] burn with his brand!
    Didst see aught of Daw?

---

18. *rives*] is split.
19. *row*] hedge.
20. *maw*] stomach, guts.

1st Shepherd.   Yea, on the pasture-land
   I heard him blow just before; he comes nigh at hand
        Below there.
   Stand still.
2nd Shepherd. Why?
1st Shepherd.   For he comes, hope I.
2nd Shepherd.   He'll catch us both with some lie
        Unless we beware.

[*The Third Shepherd enters, at first without seeing them.*]

3rd Shepherd.   Christ's cross me speed and St. Nicholas!
   Thereof in sooth I had need, it is worse than it was.
   Whoso hath knowledge, take heed, and let the world pass,
   You may never trust it, indeed, — it's as brittle as glass,
        As it rangeth.
   Never before fared this world so,
   With marvels that greater grow,
   Now in weal, now in woe,
        And everything changeth.

   There was never since Noah's flood such floods seen,
   Winds and rains so rude and storms so keen;
   Some stammered, some stood in doubt, as I ween.[21] —
   Now God turn all to good, I say as I mean!
        For ponder
   How these floods all drown
   Both in fields and in town,
   And bear all down,
        And that is a wonder!

   We that walk of nights our cattle to keep,

[*Catches sight of the others.*]

   We see startling sights when other men sleep.
   Yet my heart grows more light — I see shrews[22] a-peep.
   Ye are two tall wights[23] — I will give my sheep
        A turn, below.
   But my mood is ill-sent;
   As I walk on this bent,[24]

---

21. *ween*] suppose, imagine.
22. *shrews*] rascals.
23. *wights*] creatures.
24. *bent*] unenclosed pasture, heath.

I may lightly repent,
     If I stub my toe.
Ah, Sir, God you save and my master sweet!
A drink I crave, and somewhat to eat.
1st Shepherd.   Christ's curse, my knave, thou 'rt a lazy cheat!
2nd Shepherd.   Lo, the boy lists[25] to rave! Wait till later for meat,
     We have eat it.
Ill thrift on thy pate!
Though the rogue came late,
Yet is he in state
     To eat, could he get it.
3rd Shepherd.   That such servants as I, that sweat and swink,[26]
Eat our bread full dry gives me reason to think.
Wet and weary we sigh while our masters wink,[27]
Yet full late we come by our dinner and drink —
     But soon thereto
Our dame and sire,
When we've run in the mire,
Take a nip from our hire,
     And pay slow as they care to.

But hear my oath, master, since you find fault this way,
I shall do this hereafter — work to fit my pay;
I'll do just so much, sir, and now and then play,
For never yet supper in my stomach lay
     In the fields.
But why dispute so?
Off with staff I can go.
"Easy bargain," men say,
     "But a poor return yields."
1st Shepherd.   Thou wert an ill lad for work to ride wooing
From a man that had but little for spending.[28]
2nd Shepherd.   Peace, boy, I bade! No more jangling,
    Or I'll make thee full sad, by the Heaven's King,
     With thy gauds![29]
Where are our sheep, boy? Left lorn?[30]

---

25. *lists*] wants.
26. *swink*] toil.
27. *wink*] sleep.
28. *Thou . . . spending*] You would be a bad servant for a poor man to take along when he
    goes wooing.
29. *gauds*] pranks, tricks, jokes.
30. *lorn*] lost, forlorn.

3rd Shepherd.   Sir, this same day at morn,
 I them left in the corn
   When they rang Lauds.[31]

 They have pasture good, they cannot go wrong.
1st Shepherd.   That is right. By the Rood,[32] these nights are long!
 Ere we go now, I would someone gave us a song.
2nd Shepherd.   So I thought as I stood, to beguile us along.
3rd Shepherd.   I agree.
1st Shepherd.   The tenor I'll try.
2nd Shepherd.   And I the treble so high.
3rd Shepherd.   Then the mean shall be I.
 How ye chant now, let's see!

[*They sing (the song is not given).*]
[*Tunc entrat Mak, in clamide se super togam vestitus.*][33]

Mak.   Now, Lord, by thy seven names' spell, that made both moon and
  stars on high,
 Full more than I can tell, by thy will for me, Lord, lack I.
 I am all at odds, nought goes well — that oft doth my temper try.
 Now would God I might in heaven dwell, for there no children cry,
   So still.
1st Shepherd.   Who is that pipes so poor?
Mak.   Would God ye knew what I endure!
1st Shepherd.   Lo, a man that walks on the moor,
  And has not all his will!
2nd Shepherd.   Mak, whither dost speed? What news do you bring?
3rd Shepherd.   Is he come? Then take heed each one to his thing.

[*Et accipit clamiden ab ipso.*][34]

Mak.   What! I am a yeoman — since there's need I should tell you — of
  the King,
 That self-same, indeed, messenger from a great lording,
   And the like thereby.
 Fie on you! Go hence
 Out of my presence!
 I must have reverence,
   And you ask "who am I!"

---

31. *Lauds*] The first of the canonical hours of daily service.
32. *Rood*] Cross.
33. *Tunc . . . vestitus*] A stage direction in the original manuscript: "Then enters Mak, who
 has put on a cloak above his ordinary dress."
34. *Et . . . ipso*] Another original stage direction: "And takes the cloak off him."

1st Shepherd.   Why dress ye it up so quaint? Mak, ye do ill!
2nd Shepherd.   But, Mak, listen, ye saint, I believe what ye will!
3rd Shepherd.   I trow the knave can feint, by the neck the devil him
    kill!
Mak.   I shall make complaint, and you'll all get your fill,
            At a word from me —
    And tell your doings, forsooth!
1st Shepherd.   But, Mak, is that truth?
    Now take out that southern tooth[35]
            And stick in a flea!
2nd Shepherd.   Mak, the devil be in your eye, verily! to a blow I'd fain
    treat you.
3rd Shepherd.   Mak, know you not me? By God, I could beat you!
Mak.   God keep you all three! Me thought I had seen you — I greet
    you,
    Ye are a fair company!
1st Shepherd.   Oh, now you remember, you cheat, you!
2nd Shepherd.   Shrew, jokes are cheap!
    When thus late a man goes,
    What will folk suppose? —
    You've a bad name, God knows,
            For stealing of sheep!
Mak.   And true as steel am I, all men know and say,
    But a sickness I feel, verily, that grips me hard, night and day.
    My belly is all awry, it is out of play —
3rd Shepherd.   "Seldom doth the Devil lie dead by the way[36] —"
Mak.   Therefore
    Full sore am I and ill,
    Though I stand stone still;
    I've not eat a needle[37]
            This month and more.
1st Shepherd.   How fares thy wife, by my hood, how fares she, ask I?
Mak.   Lies asprawl, by the Rood, lo, the fire close by,
    And a house-full of home-brewed she drinks full nigh —
    Ill may speed any good thing that she will try
            Else to do!
    Eats as fast as may be,

---

35. *Now . . . tooth*] Now stop talking like a southerner.
36. *"Seldom . . . way"*] An old proverb: "The devil is always on the move."
37. *needle*] a little bit.

And each year there'll a day be
She brings forth a baby,
  And some years two.

But were I now kinder, d'ye hear, and far richer in purse,
Still were I eaten clear out of house and home, sirs.
And she's a foul-favored dear, see her close, by God's curse!
No one knows or may hear, I trow, of a worse,
  Not any!
Now will ye see what I proffer? —
To give all in my coffer,
To-morrow next to offer
  Her head-mass penny.[38]

2nd Shepherd. Faith, so weary and worn is there none in this shire.
I must sleep, were I shorn of a part of my hire.
3rd Shepherd. I'm naked, cold, and forlorn, and would fain have a fire.
1st Shepherd. I'm clean spent, for, since morn, I've run in the mire.
  Watch thou, do!
2nd Shepherd. Nay, I'll lie down hereby,
 For I must sleep, truly.
3rd Shepherd. As good a man's son was I,
  As any of you!

[*They prepare to lie down.*]

But, Mak, come lie here in between, if you please.
Mak. You'll be hindered, I fear, from talking at ease,
  Indeed!

[*He yields and lies down.*]

   From my top to my toe,
   Manus tuas commendo.
   Poncio Pilato.[39]
  Christ's cross me speed!

[*Tunc surgit, pastoribus dormientibus, et dicit:*][40]

Now 't were time a man knew, that lacks what he'd fain hold,
To steal privily through then into a fold,
And then nimbly his work do — and be not too bold,

---

38. *head-mass penny*] penny paid for a mass said for a dead person.
39. *Manus . . . Pilato*] "I commend thy hands to Pontius Pilate." (a garbled quotation).
40. *Tunc . . . dicit:*] Original stage direction: "Then he rises, when the shepherds are asleep, and says:"

For his bargain he'd rue, if it were told
        At the ending
Now 't were time their wrath to tell! —
But he needs good counsel
That fain would fare well,
        And has but little for spending.

But about you a circle as round as a moon,

[*He draws the circle.*][41]

Till I have done what I will, till that it be noon,
That ye lie stone still, until I have done;
And I shall say thereto still, a few good words soon
        Of might:
Over your heads my hand I lift.
Out go your eyes! Blind be your sight!
But I must make still better shift,
        If it's to be right.

Lord, how hard they sleep — that may ye all hear!
I never herded sheep, but I'll learn now, that's clear.
Though the flock be scared a heap, yet shall I slip near.

[*He captures a sheep.*]

Hey — hitherward creep! Now that betters our cheer
        From sorrow.
A fat sheep, I dare say!
A good fleece, swear I may!
When I can, then I'll pay,
        But this I will borrow!

[*Mak goes to his house, and knocks at the door.*]

Mak.   Ho, Gill, art thou in? Get us a light!
Gill.   Who makes such a din at this time of night?
I am set for to spin, I think not I might
Rise a penny to win! Curses loud on them light
        Trouble cause!
A busy house-wife all day
To be called thus away!
No work's done, I say,
        Because of such small chores!
Mak.   The door open, good Gill. See'st thou not what I bring?

41. *He . . . circle*] Mak is casting a spell on the three shepherds.

Gill.   Draw the latch, an thou will. Ah, come in, my sweeting!
Mak.   Yea, thou need'st not care didst thou kill me with such long
            standing!
Gill.   By the naked neck still thou art likely to swing.
Mak.   Oh, get away!
          I am worthy of my meat,
          For at a pinch I can get
          More than they that swink and sweat
                    All the long day.

          Thus it fell to my lot, Gill! Such luck came my way!
Gill.   It were a foul blot to be hanged for it some day.
Mak.   I have often escaped, Gillot, as risky a play.
Gill.   But "though long goes the pot to the water," men say,
                "At last
          Comes it home broken."
Mak.   Well know I the token,
          But let it never be spoken —
                    But come and help fast!

          I would he were slain, I would like well to eat,
          This twelvemonth was I not so fain to have some sheep's meat.
Gill.   Should they come ere he's slain and hear the sheep bleat —
Mak.   Then might I be ta'en. That were a cold sweat!
                The door —
          Go close it!
Gill.   Yes, Mak, —
          For if they come at thy back —
Mak.   Then might I suffer from the whole pack
                The devil, and more!
Gill.   A good trick have I spied, since thou thinkest of none,
          Here shall we him hide until they be gone —
          In my cradle he'll bide — just you let me alone —
          And I shall lie beside in childbed and groan.
Mak.   Well said!
          And I shall say that this night
          A boy child saw the light.
Gill.   Now that day was bright
                That saw me born and bred!

          This is a good device and a far cast.[42]

---

42. *a far cast*] a far-fetched (clever) trick.

Ever a woman's advice gives help at the last!
I care not who spies! Now go thou back fast!
Mak.   Save[43] I come ere they rise, there'll blow a cold blast!

[*Mak goes back to the moor, and prepares to lie down.*]
                    I will go sleep.
          Still sleeps all this company,
          And I shall slip in privily
          As it had never been I
                    That carried off their sheep.
1st Shepherd.   Resurrex a mortruis![44] Reach me a hand!
          Judas carnas dominus![45] I can hardly stand!
          My foot's asleep, by Jesus, and my mouth's dry as sand.
          I thought we had laid us full nigh to England!
2nd Shepherd.   Yea, verily!
          Lord, but I have slept well.
          As fresh as an eel,
          As light do I feel,
                    As leaf on the tree.
3rd Shepherd.   Ben'cite be herein! So my body is quaking,
          My heart is out of my skin with the to-do it's making.
          Who's making all this din, so my head's set to aching.
          To the doer I'll win! Hark, you fellows, be waking!
                    Four we were —
          See ye aught of Mak now?
1st Shepherd.   We were up ere thou.
2nd Shepherd.   Man, to God I vow,
                    Not once did he stir.
3rd Shepherd.   Methought he was lapt in a wolf's skin.
1st Shepherd.   So many are wrapped now — namely within.
3rd Shepherd.   When we had long napped, methought with a gin[46]
          A fat sheep he trapped, but he made no din.
2nd Shepherd.   Be still!
          Thy dream makes thee mad,
          It's a nightmare you 've had.
1st Shepherd.   God bring good out of bad,
                    If it be his will!
2nd Shepherd.   Rise, Mak, for shame! Right long dost thou lie.

---

43. *Save*] Unless.
44. *Resurrex a mortruis!*] Risen from the dead (garbled Latin).
45. *Judas carnas dominus!*] Judas killer of the Lord (??) (garbled Latin).
46. *gin*] snare.

Mak.   Now Christ's Holy Name be with us for aye!
    What's this, by Saint James, I can't move when I try.
    I suppose I'm the same. Oo-o, my neck's lain awry
          Enough, perdie —
    Many thanks! — since yester even.
    Now, by Saint Stephen,
    I was plagued by a sweven,[47]
          Knocked the heart of me.

    I thought Gill begun to croak and travail full sad,[48]
    Well-nigh at the first cock, with a young lad
    To add to our flock. Of that I am never glad,
    I have "tow on my rock[49] more than ever I had."
          Oh, my head!
    A house full of young banes[50] —
    The devil knock out their brains!
    Wo is him many gains,
          And thereto little bread.

    I must go home, by your leave, to Gill, as I thought.
    Prithee look in my sleeve that I steal naught.
    I am loath you to grieve, or from you take aught.
3rd Shepherd.   Go forth — ill may'st thou thrive!   [*Mak goes.*]
                    Now I would that we sought
        This morn,
    That we had all our store.
1st Shepherd.   But I will go before.
    Let us meet.
2nd Shepherd.   Where, Daw?
3rd Shepherd.   At the crooked thorn.

[*They go out. Mak enters and knocks at his door.*]

Mak.   Undo the door, see who's here! How long must I stand?
Gill.   Who's making such gear? Now "walk in the wenyand."[51]
Mak.   Ah, Gill, what cheer? It is I, Mak, your husband.
Gill.   Then may we "see here the devil in a band,"
        Sir Guile!
    Lo, he comes with a note

---

47. *sweven*] dream.
48. *sad*] hard.
49. *tow on my rock*] flax on my distaff; trouble.
50. *banes*] curses, pests (i.e., his children).
51. *wenyand*] waning of the moon (considered an unlucky time).

As he were held by the throat.
And I cannot devote
    To my work any while.
Mak.   Will ye hear the pother she makes to get her a gloze[52] —
Naught but pleasure she takes, and curls up her toes.
Gill.   Why, who runs, who wakes,[53] who comes, who goes,
Who brews, who bakes, what makes me hoarse, d'ye suppose!
    And also,
It is ruth to behold,
Now in hot, now in cold,
Full woeful is the household
    That no woman doth know!

But what end hast thou made with the shepherds, Mak?
Mak.   The last word that they said when I turned my back
Was they'd see that they had of their sheep all the pack.
They'll not be pleased, I'm afraid, when they their sheep lack,
    Perdie.
But how so the game go,
They'll suspect me, whether or no,
And raise a great bellow,
    And cry out upon me.

But thou must use thy sleight.
Gill.   Yea, I think it not ill.
I shall swaddle him aright in my cradle with skill.
Were it yet a worse plight, yet a way I'd find still.

[*Gill meanwhile swaddles the sheep and places him in the cradle.*]

I will lie down forthright.[54] Come tuck me up.
Mak.   That I will.
Gill.   Behind!

[*Mak tucks her in at the back.*]

If Coll come and his marrow,[55]
They will nip us full narrow.
Mak.   But I may cry out "Haro,"[56]
    The sheep if they find.

---

52. *gloze*] excuse.
53. *wakes*] watches (through the night).
54. *forthright*] right away, immediately.
55. *marrow*] company, companion, mate.
56. *"Haro"*] "Woe's me! Help!"

Gill.   Hearken close till they call — they will come anon.
        Come and make ready all, and sing thou alone —
        Sing lullaby, thou shalt, for I must groan
        And cry out by the wall on Mary and John
                Full sore.
        Sing lullaby on fast,
        When thou hear'st them at last,
        And, save I play a shrewd cast,[57]
                Trust me no more.

[*The Shepherds enter on the moor and meet.*]

3rd Shepherd.   Ah, Coll, good morn! Why sleepest thou not?
1st Shepherd.   Alas, that ever I was born! We have a foul blot.
        A fat wether have we lorn.[58]
3rd Shepherd.   Marry, God forbid, say it not!
2nd Shepherd.   Who should do us that scorn?[59] That were a foul spot.
1st Shepherd.   Some shrew.[60]
        I have sought with my dogs
        All Horbury Shrogs,[61]
        And of fifteen hogs[62]
                Found I all but one ewe.
3rd Shepherd.   Now trust me, if you will, by Saint Thomas of Kent,
        Either Mak or Gill their aid thereto lent!
1st Shepherd.   Peace, man, be still! I saw when he went.
        Thou dost slander him ill. Thou shouldest repent
                At once, indeed!
2nd Shepherd.   So may I thrive, perdie,
        Should I die here where I be,
        I would say it was he
                That did that same deed!
3rd Shepherd.   Go we thither, quick sped, and run on our feet,
        I shall never eat bread till I know all complete!
1st Shepherd.   Nor drink in my head till with him I meet.
2nd Shepherd.   In no place will I bed until I him greet,
                My brother!
        One vow I will plight,

---

57. *cast*] trick.
58. *A . . . lorn*] A fat ram have we lost.
59. *scorn*] evil trick.
60. *shrew*] rascal.
61. *Shrogs*] Thickets.
62. *hogs*] young sheep.

Till I see him in sight,
I will ne'er sleep one night
          Where I do another!

[*They go to Mak's house. Mak, hearing them coming, begins to sing lullaby at the top of his voice, while Gill groans in concert.*]

3rd Shepherd.   Hark the row they make! List our sire there croon![63]
1st Shepherd.   Never heard I voice break so clear out of tune.
     Call to him.
2nd Shepherd.   Mak, wake there! Undo your door soon!
Mak.   Who is that spake as if it were noon?
          Aloft?
     Who is that, I say?
3rd Shepherd.   Good fellows, if it were day —   [*Mocking Mak.*]
Mak.   As far as ye may,
                    Kindly, speak soft;

O'er a sick woman's head in such grievous throes!
I were liefer dead[64] than she should suffer such woes.
Gill.   Go elsewhere, well sped. Oh, how my pain grows —
     Each footfall ye tread goes straight through my nose
               So loud, woe's me!
1st Shepherd.   Tell us, Mak, if ye may,
     How fare ye, I say?
Mak.   But are ye in this town to-day —
          Now how fare ye?

Ye have run in the mire and are wet still a bit,
I will make you a fire, if ye will sit.
A nurse I would hire — can you help me in it?
Well quit is my hire — my dream the truth hit —
          In season.
I have bairns, if ye knew,
Plenty more than will do,
But we must drink as we brew,
          And that is but reason.

I would ye would eat ere ye go. Methinks that ye sweat.
2nd Shepherd.   Nay, no help could we know in what's drunken or eat.

---

63. *List . . . croon!*] Our sire wants (lists) to sing.
64. *I . . . dead*] I would rather be dead.

Mak.   Why, sir, ails you aught but good, though?
3rd Shepherd.   Yea, our sheep that we get
    Are stolen as they go; our loss is great.
Mak.   Sirs, drink!
    Had I been there,
    Some one had bought it sore, I swear.
1st Shepherd.   Marry, some men trow that ye were,
        And that makes us think!
2nd Shepherd.   Mak, one and another trows it should be ye.
3rd Shepherd.   Either ye or your spouse, so say we.
Mak.   Now if aught suspicion throws on Gill or me,
    Come and search our house, and then may ye see
        Who had her —
    If I any sheep got,
    Or cow or stot;[65]
    And Gill, my wife, rose not,
        Here since we laid her.

    As I am true and leal,[66] to God, here I pray
    That this is the first meal that I shall eat this day.
1st Shepherd.   Mak, as may I have weal,[67] advise thee, I say —
    "He learned timely to steal that could not say nay."
Gill.   Me, my death you've dealt!
    Out, ye thieves, nor come again,
    Ye've come just to rob us, that's plain.
Mak.   Hear ye not how she groans amain —
        Your hearts should melt!
Gill.   From my child, thieves, begone. Go nigh him not, — there's the
      door!
Mak.   If ye knew all she's borne, your hearts would be sore.
    Ye do wrong, I you warn, thus to come in before
    A woman that has borne — but I say no more.
Gill.   Oh, my middle — I die!
    I vow to God so mild,
    If ever I you beguiled,
    That I will eat this child
        That doth in this cradle lie!
Mak.   Peace, woman, by God's pain, and cry not so.
    Thou dost hurt thy brain and fill me with woe.

---

65. *stot*] bullock.
66. *leal*] just.
67. *weal*] prosperity, happiness.

2nd Shepherd.   I trow our sheep is slain. What find ye two, though?
        Our work's all in vain. We may as well go.
                    Save clothes and such matters
        I can find no flesh
        Hard or nesh,
        Salt nor fresh,
                    Except two empty platters.
        Of any "cattle"[68] but this, tame or wild, that we see,
        None, as may I have bliss, smelled as loud as he.[69]
Gill.   No, so God joy and bliss of my child may give me!
1st Shepherd.   We have aimed amiss; deceived, I trow, were we.
2nd Shepherd.   Sir, wholly each, one.
        Sir, Our Lady him save!
        Is your child a knave?[70]
Mak.   Any lord might him have,
                    This child, for his son.

        When he wakes, so he grips, it's a pleasure to see.
3rd Shepherd.   Good luck to his hips, and blessing, say we!
        But who were his gossips,[71] now tell who they be?
Mak.   Blest be their lips —   [*Hesitates, at a loss.*]
1st Shepherd.   Hark a lie now, trust me!   [*Aside.*]
Mak.   So may God them thank,
        Parkin and Gibbon Waller, I say,
        And gentle John Horn, in good fey[72] —
        He made all the fun and play —
                    With the great shank.[73]
2nd Shepherd.   Mak, friends will we be, for we are at one.
Mak.   We — nay, count not on me, for amends get I none.
        Farewell, all three! Glad 't will be when ye 're gone!

[*The Shepherds go.*]

3rd Shepherd.   "Fair words there may be, but love there is none
                    This year."
1st Shepherd.   Gave ye the child anything?
2nd Shepherd.   I trow, not one farthing.

---

68. *"cattle"*] livestock.
69. *he*] the "baby."
70. *knave*] boy.
71. *gossips*] sponsors, godparents.
72. *fey*] faith.
73. *shank*] long legs.

3rd Shepherd.   Fast back I will fling.
        Await ye me here.

[*Daw goes back. The other Shepherds turn and follow him slowly, entering while he is talking with Mak.*]

3rd Shepherd.   Mak, I trust thou'lt not grieve, if I go to thy child.
Mak.   Nay, great hurt I receive, — thou hast acted full wild.
3rd Shepherd.   Thy bairn 't will not grieve, little day-star so mild.
    Mak, by your leave, let me give your child
        But six-pence.

[*Daw goes to cradle, and starts to draw away the covering.*]

Mak.   Nay, stop it — he sleeps!
3rd Shepherd.   Methinks he peeps —
Mak.   When he wakens, he weeps;
        I pray you go hence!

[*The other Shepherds return.*]

3rd Shepherd.   Give me leave him to kiss, and lift up the clout.[74]
    What the devil is this? — he has a long snout!
1st Shepherd.   He's birth-marked amiss. We waste time hereabout.
2nd Shepherd.   "A weft that ill-spun is comes ever foul out."
                        [*He sees the sheep.*]
            Aye — so!
    He is like to our sheep!
3rd Shepherd.   Ho, Gib, may I peep?
1st Shepherd.   I trow "Nature will creep
        Where it may not go."
2nd Shepherd.   This was a quaint gaud[75] and a far cast.
    It was a high fraud.
    3rd Shepherd.   Yea, sirs, that was 't.
Let's burn this bawd, and bind her fast.
"A false scold," by the Lord, "will hang at the last!"
    So shalt thou!
Will ye see how they swaddle
His four feet in the middle!
Saw I never in the cradle
    A horned lad ere now!
Mak.   Peace, I say! Tell ye what, this to-do ye can spare!

---

74. *clout*] cloth.
75. *quaint gaud*] strange, shrewd trick.

[*Pretending anger.*]

It was I him begot and yon woman him bare.
1st Shepherd.   What the devil for name has he got? Mak? —
Lo, God, Mak's heir!
2nd Shepherd.   Come, joke with him not. Now, may God give him
care, I say!
Gill.   A pretty child is he
As sits on a woman's knee,
A dilly-down,[76] perdie,
To make a man gay.
3rd Shepherd.   I know him by the ear-mark — that is a good token.
Mak.   I tell you, sirs, hark, his nose was broken —
Then there told me a clerk he'd been mis-spoken.[77]
1st Shepherd.   Ye deal falsely and dark; I would fain be wroken.[78]
Get a weapon, — go!
Gill.   He was taken by an elf,
I saw it myself.
When the clock struck twelve,
Was he mis-shapen[79] so.
2nd Shepherd.   Ye two are at one, that's plain, in all ye 've done and
said.
1st Shepherd.   Since their theft they maintain, let us leave them dead!
Mak.   If I trespass again, strike off my head!
At your will I remain.
3rd Shepherd.   Sirs, take my counsel instead.
For this trespass
We'll neither curse nor wrangle in spite,
Chide nor fight,
But have done forthright,
And toss him in canvas.

[*They toss Mak in one of Gill's canvas sheets till they are tired. He
disappears groaning into his house. The Shepherds pass over to the moor
on the other side of the stage.*]

1st Shepherd.   Lord, lo! but I am sore, like to burst, in back and breast.
In faith, I may no more, therefore will I rest.
2nd Shepherd.   Like a sheep of seven score he weighed in my fist.
To sleep anywhere, therefore seemeth now best.

---

76. *dilly-down*] darling.
77. *mis-spoken*] bewitched.
78. *wroken*] revenged.
79. *mis-shapen*] transformed.

3rd Shepherd.   Now I you pray,
     On this green let us lie.
1st Shepherd.   O'er those thieves yet chafe I.
3rd Shepherd.   Let your anger go by, —
                    Come do as I say.

[*As they are about to lie down the Angel appears.*]
[*Angelus cantat "Gloria in excelsis." Postea dicat:*][80]

Angel.   Rise, herdsmen gentle, attend ye, for now is he born
          From the fiend that shall rend what Adam had lorn,
          That warlock to shend,[81] this night is he born,
          God is made your friend now on this morn.
                    Lo! thus doth he command —
          Go to Bethlehem, see
          Where he lieth so free,[82]
          In a manger full lowly
                    'Twixt where twain[83] beasts stand.

[*The Angel goes.*]

1st Shepherd.   This was a fine voice, even as ever I heard.
     It is a marvel, by St. Stephen, thus with dread to be stirred.
2nd Shepherd.   'Twas of God's Son from heaven he these tidings
          averred.
     All the wood with a levin,[84] methought at his word
                    Shone fair.
3rd Shepherd.   Of a Child did he tell,
     In Bethlehem, mark ye well.
1st Shepherd.   That this star yonder doth spell —
                    Let us seek him there.
2nd Shepherd.   Say, what was his song — how it went, did ye hear?
     Three breves[85] to a long —
3rd Shepherd.   Marry, yes, to my ear
     There was no crotchet[86] wrong, naught it lacked and full clear!
1st Shepherd.   To sing it here, us among, as he nicked it, full near,
                    I know how —

---

80. *Angelus . . . dicat:*] An original stage direction: "The Angel sings the 'Gloria in Excelsis.'
    Then let him say:"
81. *shend*] spoil, overthrow.
82. *free*] noble.
83. *twain*] two.
84. *levin*] lightning.
85. *breves*] short notes.
86. *crotchet*] note.

2nd Shepherd.   Let's see how you croon!
    Can you bark at the moon?
3rd Shepherd.   Hold your tongues, have done!
    Hark after me now!   [*They sing.*]
2nd Shepherd.   To Bethlehem he bade that we should go.
    I am sore adrad[87] that we tarry too slow.
3rd Shepherd.   Be merry, and not sad — our song's of mirth not of woe,
    To be forever glad as our meed[88] may we know,
        Without noise.
1st Shepherd.   Hie we thither, then, speedily,
    Though we be wet and weary,
    To that Child and that Lady! —
    We must not lose those joys!
2nd Shepherd.   We find by the prophecy — let be your din! —
    David and Isaiah, and more that I mind me therein,
    They prophesied by clergy, that in a virgin,
    Should he alight and lie, to assuage our sin,
        And slake it,
    Our nature, from woe,
    For it was Isaiah said so,
    "*Ecce virgo*
        Concipiet"[89] a child that is naked.
3rd Shepherd.   Full glad may we be and await that day
    That lovesome one to see, that all mights doth sway.
    Lord, well it were with me, now and for aye,
    Might I kneel on my knee some word for to say
        To that child.
    But the angel said
    In a crib was he laid,
    He was poorly arrayed,
        Both gracious and mild.
1st Shepherd.   Patriarchs that have been and prophets beforne,[90]
    They desired to have seen this child that is born.
    They are gone full clean, — that have they lorn.
    We shall see him, I ween, ere it be morn,
        For token.[91]
    When I see him and feel,
    I shall know full well,

87. *adrad*] adread, afraid.
88. *meed*] reward.
89. *"Ecce virgo Concipiet"*] "Behold, a virgin shall conceive." (Isaiah 7:14).
90. *beforne*] before.
91. *For token*] As a sign.

It is true as steel,
What prophets have spoken,

To so poor as we are that he would appear,
First find and declare by his messenger.
2nd Shepherd.   Go we now, let us fare, the place is us near.
3rd Shepherd.   I am ready and eager to be there; let us together with
cheer
To that bright one go.
Lord, if thy will it be,
Untaught are we all three,
Some kind of joy grant us, that we
Thy creatures, comfort may know!

[*They enter the stable and adore the infant Saviour.*]

1st Shepherd.   Hail, thou comely and clean one! Hail, young Child!
Hail, Maker, as I mean, from a maiden so mild!
Thou hast harried, I ween, the warlock so wild, —
The false beguiler with his teen[92] now goes beguiled.
Lo, he merries,
Lo, he laughs, my sweeting!
A happy meeting!
Here's my promised greeting, —
Have a bob of cherries!
2nd Shepherd.   Hail, sovereign Saviour, for thou hast us sought!
Hail, noble nursling and flower, that all things hast wrought!
Hail, thou, full of gracious power, that made all from nought!
Hail, I kneel and I cower! A bird have I brought
To my bairn from far.
Hail, little tiny mop![93]
Of our creed thou art the crop,[94]
I fain would drink in thy cup,
Little day-star!
3rd Shepherd.   Hail, darling dear one, full of Godhead indeed!
I pray thee be near, when I have need.
Hail, sweet is thy cheer! My heart would bleed
To see thee sit here in so poor a weed,[95]
With no pennies.
Hail, put forth thy dall,[96]

92. *teen*] vexation, pain, grief.
93. *mop*] baby.
94. *crop*] head, topmost part.
95. *weed*] dress, covering.
96. *dall*] fist.

I bring thee but a ball,
Keep it, and play with it withal,
      And go to the tennis.

Mary.   The Father of Heaven this night, God omnipotent,
That setteth all things aright, his Son hath he sent.
My name he named and did light on me ere that he went.
I conceived him forthright through his might as he meant,
      And now he is born.
May he keep you from woe!
I shall pray him do so.
Tell it, forth as ye go,
      And remember this morn.

1st Shepherd.   Farewell, Lady, so fair to behold
With thy child on thy knee!
   2nd Shepherd.   But he lies full cold!
Lord, 't is well with me! Now we go, behold!

3rd Shepherd.   Forsooth, already it seems to be told
      Full oft!
1st Shepherd.   What grace we have found!
2nd Shepherd.   Now are we won safe and sound.
3rd Shepherd.   Come forth, to sing are we bound.
      Make it ring then aloft!

[*They depart singing.*]

Explicit pagina Pastorum.[97]

---

97. *Explicit . . . Pastorum.*] Here endeth the play of the Shepherds.

EVERYMAN

CHARACTERS

EVERYMAN	STRENGTH
GOD: ADONAI	DISCRETION
DEATH	FIVE-WITS
MESSENGER	BEAUTY
FELLOWSHIP	KNOWLEDGE
COUSIN	CONFESSION
KINDRED	ANGEL
GOODS	DOCTOR
GOOD-DEEDS	

HERE BEGINNETH A TREATISE HOW THE HIGH FATHER OF HEAVEN
· SENDETH DEATH TO SUMMON EVERY CREATURE TO COME AND
GIVE ACCOUNT OF THEIR LIVES IN THIS WORLD AND IS IN MAN-
NER OF A MORAL PLAY.

Messenger.   I pray you all give your audience,
    And hear this matter with reverence,
    By figure a moral play —
    The *Summoning of Everyman* called it is,
    That of our lives and ending shows
    How transitory we be all day.
    This matter is wondrous precious,
    But the intent of it is more gracious,
    And sweet to bear away.
    The story saith, — Man, in the beginning,
    Look well, and take good heed to the ending,
    Be you never so gay!

Ye think sin in the beginning full sweet,
Which in the end causeth thy soul to weep,
When the body lieth in clay.
Here shall you see how *Fellowship* and *Jollity*,
Both *Strength*, *Pleasure*, and *Beauty*,
Will fade from thee as flower in May.
For ye shall hear, how our heaven king
Calleth *Everyman* to a general reckoning:
Give audience, and hear what he doth say.

God.   I perceive here in my majesty,
How that all creatures be to me unkind,
Living without dread in worldly prosperity:
Of ghostly sight the people be so blind,
Drowned in sin, they know me not for their God;
In worldly riches is all their mind,
They fear not my rightwiseness, the sharp rod;
My law that I shewed, when I for them died,
They forget clean, and shedding of my blood red;
I hanged between two, it cannot be denied;
To get them life I suffered to be dead;
I healed their feet, with thorns hurt was my head:
I could do no more than I did truly,
And now I see the people do clean forsake me.
They use the seven deadly sins damnable;
As pride, covetise, wrath, and lechery,
Now in the world be made commendable;
And thus they leave of angels the heavenly company;
Everyman liveth so after his own pleasure,
And yet of their life they be nothing sure:
I see the more that I them forbear
The worse they be from year to year;
All that liveth appaireth[1] fast,
Therefore I will in all the haste
Have a reckoning of Everyman's person
For and[2] I leave the people thus alone
In their life and wicked tempests,
Verily they will become much worse than beasts;
For now one would by envy another up eat;
Charity they all do clean forget.
I hoped well that Everyman

---

1. *appaireth*] is impaired, degenerates.
2. *and*] if.

In my glory should make his mansion,
And thereto I had them all elect;
But now I see, like traitors deject,
They thank me not for the pleasure that I to them meant,
Nor yet for their being that I them have lent;
I proffered the people great multitude of mercy,
And few there be that asketh it heartily;
They be so cumbered with worldly riches,
That needs on them I must do justice,
On Everyman living without fear.
Where art thou, *Death*, thou mighty messenger?

Death.   Almighty God, I am here at your will,
Your commandment to fulfil.

God.   Go thou to *Everyman*,
And show him in my name
A pilgrimage he must on him take,
Which he in no wise may escape;
And that he bring with him a sure reckoning
Without delay or any tarrying.

Death.   Lord, I will in the world go run over all,
And cruelly outsearch both great and small;
Every man will I beset that liveth beastly
Out of God's laws, and dreadeth not folly:
He that loveth riches I will strike with my dart,
His sight to blind, and from heaven to depart,
Except that alms be his good friend,
In hell for to dwell, world without end.
Lo, yonder I see *Everyman* walking;
Full little he thinketh on my coming;
His mind is on fleshly lusts and his treasure,
And great pain it shall cause him to endure
Before the Lord Heaven King.
Everyman, stand still; whither art thou going
Thus gaily? Hast thou thy Maker forget?

Everyman.   Why askst thou?
Wouldest thou wete?[3]

Death.   Yea, sir, I will show you;
In great haste I am sent to thee
From God out of his majesty.

Everyman.   What, sent to me?

Death.   Yea, certainly.
Though thou have forget him here,

3. *wete*] wit, i.e., know.

He thinketh on thee in the heavenly sphere,
As, or[4] we depart, thou shalt know.
Everyman.   What desireth God of me?
Death.   That shall I show thee;
A reckoning he will needs have
Without any longer respite.
Everyman.   To give a reckoning longer leisure I crave;
This blind[5] matter troubleth my wit.
Death.   On thee thou must take a long journey:
Therefore thy book of count with thee thou bring;
For turn again thou can not by no way,
And look thou be sure of thy reckoning:
For before God thou shalt answer, and show
Thy many bad deeds and good but a few;
How thou hast spent thy life, and in what wise,
Before the chief lord of paradise.
Have ado that we were in that way,[6]
For, wete thou well, thou shalt make none attournay.[7]
Everyman.   Full unready I am such reckoning to give.
I know thee not: what messenger art thou?
Death.   I am *Death*, that no man dreadeth.
For every man I rest and no man spareth;
For it is God's commandment
That all to me should be obedient.
Everyman.   O *Death*, thou comest when I had thee least in mind;
In thy power it lieth me to save,
Yet of my good will I give thee, if ye will be kind,
Yea, a thousand pound shalt thou have,
And defer this matter till another day.
Death.   *Everyman*, it may not be by no way;
I set not by gold, silver, nor riches,
Ne[8] by pope, emperor, king, duke, ne princes.
For and I would receive gifts great,
All the world I might get;
But my custom is clean contrary.
I give thee no respite: come hence, and not tarry.
Everyman.   Alas, shall I have no longer respite?
I may say *Death* giveth no warning:

4. *or*] ere, before.
5. *blind*] dark, obscure.
6. *Have ado . . . way*] [Let's] get to the business of proceeding on our way.
7. *thou shalt . . . attournay*] you cannot make anyone your mediator.
8. *Ne*] Nor.

To think on thee, it maketh my heart sick,
For all unready is my book of reckoning.
But twelve year and I might have abiding,
My counting book I would make so clear,
That my reckoning I should not need to fear.
Wherefore, *Death*, I pray thee, for God's mercy,
Spare me till I be provided of remedy.

Death.   Thee availeth not to cry, weep, and pray:
But haste thee lightly that you were gone the journey,
And prove thy friends if thou can.
For, wete thou well, the tide abideth no man,
And in the world each living creature
For *Adam's* sin must die of nature.

Everyman.   *Death*, if I should this pilgrimage take,
And my reckoning surely make,
Show me, for saint *charity*,
Should I not come again shortly?

Death.   No, *Everyman*; and thou be once there,
Thou mayst never more come here,
Trust me verily.

Everyman.   O gracious God, in the high seat celestial,
Have mercy on me in this most need;
Shall I have no company from this vale terrestrial
Of mine acquaintance that way me to lead?

Death.   Yea, if any be so hardy,
That would go with thee and bear thee company.
Hie[9] thee that you were gone to God's magnificence,
Thy reckoning to give before his presence.
What, weenest[10] thou thy life is given thee,
And thy worldly goods also?

Everyman.   I had wend so, verily.

Death.   Nay, nay; it was but lent thee;
For as soon as thou art go,
Another awhile shall have it, and then go therefro
Even as thou hast done.
Everyman, thou art mad; thou hast thy wits five,[11]
And here on earth will not amend thy life,
For suddenly I do come.

Everyman.   O wretched caitiff, whither shall I flee,

---

9. *Hie*] Hurry, make haste.
10. *weenest*] think, suppose.
11. *thy five wits*] The five wits were commonly defined as common wit (sense), imagination, fantasy, estimation and memory.

That I might scape this endless sorrow!
Now, gentle *Death*, spare me till to-morrow,
That I may amend me
With good advisement.
Death.   Nay, thereto I will not consent,
Nor no man will I respite,
But to the heart suddenly I shall smite
Without any advisement.
And now out of thy sight I will me hie;
See thou make thee ready shortly,
For thou mayst say this is the day
That no man living may scape away.
Everyman.   Alas, I may well weep with sighs deep;
Now have I no manner of company
To help me in my journey, and me to keep;
And also my writing is full unready.
How shall I do now for to excuse me?
I would to God I had never be gete![12]
To my soul a full great profit it had be;
For now I fear pains huge and great.
The time passeth; Lord, help that all wrought;
For though I mourn it availeth nought.
The day passeth, and is almost a-go;[13]
I wot not well what for to do.
To whom were I best my complaint to make?
What, and I to *Fellowship* thereof spake,
And showed him of this sudden chance?
For in him is all mine affiance;
We have in the world so many a day
Be on good friends in sport and play.
I see him yonder, certainly;
I trust that he will bear me company;
Therefore to him will I speak to ease my sorrow.
Well met, good *Fellowship*, and good morrow!
Fellowship speaketh.   *Everyman*, good morrow by this day.
Sir, why lookest thou so piteously?
If any thing be amiss, I pray thee, me say,
That I may help to remedy.
Everyman.   Yea, good *Fellowship*, yea,
I am in great jeopardy.

12. *be gete*] been gotten, been born.
13. *a-go*] gone.

Fellowship.   My true friend, show to me your mind;
    I will not forsake thee, unto my life's end,
    In the way of good company.
Everyman.   That was well spoken, and lovingly.
Fellowship.   Sir, I must needs know your heaviness;
    I have pity to see you in any distress;
    If any have you wronged ye shall revenged be,
    Though I on the ground be slain for thee, —
    Though that I know before that I should die.
Everyman.   Verily, *Fellowship*, gramercy.[14]
Fellowship.   Tush! by thy thanks I set not a straw.
    Show me your grief, and say no more.
Everyman.   If I my heart should to you break,[15]
    And then you to turn your mind from me,
    And would not me comfort, when you hear me speak,
    Then should I ten times sorrier be.
Fellowship.   Sir, I say as I will do in deed.
Everyman.   Then be you a good friend at need:
    I have found you true here before.
Fellowship.   And so ye shall evermore;
    For, in faith, and thou go to Hell,
    I will not forsake thee by the way!
Everyman.   Ye speak like a good friend; I believe you well;
    I shall deserve it, and I may.
Fellowship.   I speak of no deserving, by this day.
    For he that will say and nothing do
    Is not worthy with good company to go;
    Therefore show me the grief of your mind,
    As to your friend most loving and kind.
Everyman.   I shall show you how it is;
    Commanded I am to go a journey,
    A long way, hard and dangerous,
    And give a strait count without delay
    Before the high judge Adonai.[16]
    Wherefore I pray you, bear me company,
    As ye have promised, in this journey.
Fellowship.   That is matter indeed! Promise is duty,
    But, and I should take such a voyage on me,
    I know it well, it should be to my pain:

14. *gramercy*] great thanks.
15. *break*] open.
16. *Adonai*] God.

Also it make me afeard, certain.
But let us take counsel here as well as we can,
For your words would fear a strong man.
Everyman.   Why, ye said, If I had need,
Ye would me never forsake, quick[17] nor dead,
Though it were to hell truly.
Fellowship.   So I said, certainly,
But such pleasures be set aside, thee sooth to say:
And also, if we took such a journey,
When should we come again?
Everyman.   Nay, never again till the day of doom.
Fellowship.   In faith, then will not I come there!
Who hath you these tidings brought?
Everyman.   Indeed, *Death* was with me here.
Fellowship.   Now, by God that all hath bought,
If *Death* were the messenger,
For no man that is living to-day
I will not go that loath journey —
Not for the father that begat me!
Everyman.   Ye promised other wise, pardie.[18]
Fellowship.   I wot well I say so truly;
And yet if thou wilt eat, and drink, and make good cheer,
Or haunt to women, the lusty company,
I would not forsake you, while the day is clear,
Trust me verily!
Everyman.   Yea, thereto ye would be ready;
To go to mirth, solace, and play,
Your mind will sooner apply
Than to bear me company in my long journey.
Fellowship.   Now, in good faith, I will not that way.
But and thou wilt murder, or any man kill,
In that I will help thee with a good will!
Everyman.   O that is a simple advice indeed!
Gentle *fellow*, help me in my necessity;
We have loved long, and now I need,
And now, gentle *Fellowship*, remember me.
Fellowship.   Whether ye have loved me or no,
By Saint John, I will not with thee go.
Everyman.   Yet I pray thee, take the labour, and do so much for me

17. *quick*] living.
18. *pardie*] par Dieu, by God.

        To bring me forward, for saint charity,
        And comfort me till I come without the town.
Fellowship.   Nay, and thou would give me a new gown,
        I will not a foot with thee go;
        But and you had tarried I would not have left thee so.
        And as now, God speed thee in thy journey,
        For from thee I will depart as fast as I may.
Everyman.   Whither away, *Fellowship*? will you forsake me?
Fellowship.   Yea, by my fay,[19] to God I betake thee.
Everyman.   Farewell, good *Fellowship*; for this my heart is sore;
        Adieu for ever, I shall see thee no more.
Fellowship.   In faith, *Everyman*, farewell now at the end;
        For you I will remember that parting is mourning.
Everyman.   Alack! shall we thus depart indeed?
        Our Lady, help, without any more comfort,
        Lo, *Fellowship* forsaketh me in my most need:
        For help in this world whither shall I resort?
        Fellowship herebefore with me would merry make;
        And now little sorrow for me doth he take.
        It is said, in prosperity men friends may find,
        Which in adversity be full unkind.
        Now whither for succour shall I flee,
        Sith that[20] *Fellowship* hath forsaken me?
        To my kinsmen I will truly,
        Praying them to help me in my necessity;
        I believe that they will do so,
        For kind will creep where it may not go.
        I will go say, for yonder I see them go.
        Where be ye now, my friends and kinsmen?
Kindred.   Here be we now at your commandment.
        Cousin, I pray you show us your intent
        In any wise, and not spare.
Cousin.   Yea, *Everyman*, and to us declare
        If ye be disposed to go any whither,
        For wete you well, we will live and die together.
Kindred.   In wealth and woe we will with you hold,
        For over his kin a man may be bold.
Everyman.   Gramercy, my friends and kinsmen kind.
        Now shall I show you the grief of my mind:
        I was commanded by a messenger,

19. *fay*] faith.
20. *Sith that*] Since, now that.

That is an high king's chief officer;
He bade me go a pilgrimage to my pain,
And I know well I shall never come again;
Also I must give a reckoning straight,
For I have a great enemy, that hath me in wait,
Which intendeth me for to hinder.

Kindred. What account is that which ye must render?
That would I know.

Everyman. Of all my works I must show
How I have lived and my days spent;
Also of ill deeds, that I have used
In my time, sith life was me lent;
And of all virtues that I have refused.
Therefore I pray you go thither with me,
To help to make mine account, for saint *charity*.

Cousin. What, to go thither? Is that the matter?
Nay, *Everyman*, I had liefer[21] fast bread and water
All this five year and more.

Everyman. Alas, that ever I was bore![22]
For now shall I never be merry
If that you forsake me.

Kindred. Ah, sir; what, ye be a merry man!
Take good heart to you, and make no moan.
But one thing I warn you, by Saint Anne,
As for me, ye shall go alone.

Everyman. My *Cousin*, will you not with me go?

Cousin. No, by our Lady; I have the cramp in my toe.
Trust not to me, for, so God me speed,
I will deceive you in your most need.

Kindred. It availeth not us to tice.[23]
Ye shall have my maid with all my heart;
She loveth to go to feasts, there to be nice,
And to dance, and abroad to start:
I will give her leave to help you in that journey,
If that you and she may agree.

Everyman. Now show me the very effect of your mind.
Will you go with me, or abide behind?

Kindred. Abide behind? yea, that I will and I may!
Therefore farewell until another day.

21. *had liefer*] would rather.
22. *bore*] born.
23. *tice*] entice.

Everyman.   How should I be merry or glad?
   For fair promises to me make,
   But when I have most need, they me forsake.
   I am deceived; that maketh me sad.
Cousin.   Cousin *Everyman*, farewell now,
   For verily I will not go with you;
   Also of mine own an unready reckoning
   I have to account; therefore I make tarrying.
   Now, God keep thee, for now I go.
Everyman.   Ah, *Jesus*, is all come hereto?
   Lo, fair words maketh fools feign;
   They promise and nothing will do certain.
   My kinsmen promised me faithfully
   For to abide with me steadfastly,
   And now fast away do they flee:
   Even so *Fellowship* promised me.
   What friend were best me of to provide?
   I lose my time here longer to abide.
   Yet in my mind a thing there is; —
   All my life I have loved riches;
   If that my good now help me might,
   He would make my heart full light.
   I will speak to him in this distress. —
   Where art thou, my *Goods* and riches?
Goods.   Who calleth me? *Everyman?* what haste thou hast!
   I lie here in corners, trussed and piled so high,
   And in chests I am locked so fast,
   Also sacked in bags, thou mayst see with thine eye,
   I cannot stir; in packs low I lie.
   What would ye have, lightly[24] me say.
Everyman.   Come hither, *Good*, in all the haste thou may,
   For of counsel I must desire thee.
Goods.   Sir, and ye in the world have trouble or adversity,
   That can I help you to remedy shortly.
Everyman.   It is another disease that grieveth me;
   In this world it is not, I tell thee so.
   I am sent for another way to go,
   To give a straight account general
   Before the highest *Jupiter* of all;
   And all my life I have had joy and pleasure in thee.

24. *lightly*] quickly.

Therefore I pray thee go with me,
For, peradventure, thou mayst before God Almighty
My reckoning help to clean and purify;
For it is said ever among,
That money maketh all right that is wrong.

Goods. Nay, *Everyman*, I sing another song,
I follow no man in such voyages;
For and I went with thee
Thou shouldst fare much the worse for me;
For because on me thou did set thy mind,
Thy reckoning I have made blotted and blind,
That thine account thou cannot make truly;
And that hast thou for the love of me.

Everyman. That would grieve me full sore,
When I should come to that fearful answer.
Up, let us go thither together.

Goods. Nay, not so, I am too brittle, I may not endure;
I will follow no man one foot, be ye sure.

Everyman. Alas, I have thee loved, and had great pleasure
All my life-days on good and treasure.

Goods. That is to thy damnation without lesing,[25]
For my love is contrary to the love everlasting.
But if thou had me loved moderately during,
As, to the poor give part of me,
Then shouldst thou not in this dolour be,
Nor in this great sorrow and care.

Everyman. Lo, now was I deceived or[26] I was ware,
And all I may wyte[27] my spending of time.

Goods. What, weenest thou that I am thine?

Everyman. I had wend so.

Goods. Nay, *Everyman*, I say no;
As for a while I was lent thee,
A season thou hast had me in prosperity;
My condition is man's soul to kill;
If I save one, a thousand I do spill;
Weenest thou that I will follow thee?
Nay, from this world, not verily.

Everyman. I had wend otherwise.

25. *without lesing*] without lying, i.e. truly.
26. *or*] ere, before.
27. *wyte*] blame.

Goods.   Therefore to thy soul *Good* is a thief;
    For when thou art dead, this is my guise[28]
    Another to deceive in the same wise
    As I have done thee, and all to his soul's reprief.[29]
Everyman.   O false *Good*, cursed thou be!
    Thou traitor to God, that hast deceived me,
    And caught me in thy snare.
Goods.   Marry, thou brought thyself in care,
    Whereof I am glad,
    I must needs laugh, I cannot be sad.
Everyman.   Ah, *Good*, thou hast had long my heartly love;
    I gave thee that which should be the Lord's above.
    But wilt thou not go with me in deed?
    I pray thee truth to say.
Goods.   No, so God me speed,
    Therefore farewell, and have good day.
Everyman.   O, to whom shall I make my moan
    For to go with me in that heavy journey?
    First *Fellowship* said he would with me gone;
    His words were very pleasant and gay,
    But afterward he left me alone.
    Then spake I to my kinsmen all in despair,
    And also they gave me words fair,
    They lacked no fair speaking,
    But all forsake me in the ending.
    Then went I to my *Goods* that I loved best,
    In hope to have comfort, but there had I least;
    For my *Goods* sharply did me tell
    That he bringeth many into hell.
    Then of myself I was ashamed,
    And so I am worthy to be blamed;
    Thus may I well myself hate.
    Of whom shall I now counsel take?
    I think that I shall never speed
    Till that I go to my *Good-Deed*,
    But alas, she is so weak,
    That she can neither go nor speak;
    Yet will I venture on her now. —
    My *Good-Deeds*, where be you?

28. *guise*] custom, practice.
29. *reprief*] reproach, blame.

Good-Deeds.   Here I lie cold in the ground;
      Thy sins hath me sore bound,
      That I cannot stir.
Everyman.   O, *Good-Deeds*, I stand in fear;
      I must you pray of counsel,
      For help now should come right well.
Good-Deeds.   *Everyman*, I have understanding
      That ye be summoned account to make
      Before *Messias*, of Jerusalem King;
      And you do by me that journey what you will I take.[30]
Everyman.   Therefore I come to you, my moan to make;
      I pray you, that ye will go with me.
Good-Deeds.   I would full fain, but I cannot stand verily.
Everyman.   Why, is there anything on you fall?[31]
Good-Deeds.   Yea, sir, I may thank you of[32] all;
      If ye had perfectly cheered me,
      Your book of account now full ready had be.
      Look, the books of your works and deeds eke;[33]
      Oh, see how they lie under the feet,
      To your soul's heaviness.
Everyman.   Our Lord *Jesus*, help me!
      For one letter here I can not see.
Good-Deeds.   There is a blind reckoning in time of distress!
Everyman.   *Good-Deeds*, I pray you, help me in this need,
      Or else I am for ever damned indeed;
      Therefore help me to make reckoning
      Before the redeemer of all thing,
      That king is, and was, and ever shall.
Good-Deeds.   *Everyman*, I am sorry of your fall,
      And fain would I help you, and I were able.
Everyman.   *Good-Deeds*, your counsel I pray you give me.
Good-Deeds.   That shall I do verily;
      Though that on my feet I may not go,
      I have a sister, that shall with you also,
      Called *Knowledge*, which shall with you abide,
      To help you to make that dreadful reckoning.
Knowledge.   *Everyman*, I will go with thee, and be thy guide,
      In thy most need to go by thy side.

30. *And you . . . I take.*] If you do as I say, I will take that journey with you.
31. *fall*] befallen.
32. *of*] for.
33. *eke*] also.

Everyman.   In good condition I am now in every thing,
     And am wholly content with this good thing;
     Thanked be God my Creator.
Good-Deeds.   And when he hath brought thee there,
     Where thou shalt heal thee of thy smart,
     Then go you with your reckoning and your *Good-Deeds* together
     For to make you joyful at heart
     Before the blessed Trinity.
Everyman.   My *Good-Deeds*, gramercy;
     I am well content, certainly,
     With your words sweet.
Knowledge.   Now go we together lovingly,
     To *Confession*, that cleansing river.
Everyman.   For joy I weep; I would we were there;
     But, I pray you, give me cognition
     Where dwelleth that holy man, *Confession*.
Knowledge.   In the house of salvation:
     We shall find him in that place,
     That shall us comfort by God's grace.
     Lo, this is *Confession*; kneel down and ask mercy,
     For he is in good conceit[34] with God almighty.
Everyman.   O glorious fountain that all uncleanness doth clarify,
     Wash from me the spots of vices unclean,
     That on me no sin may be seen;
     I come with *Knowledge* for my redemption,
     Repent with hearty and full contrition;
     For I am commanded a pilgrimage to take,
     And great accounts before God to make.
     Now, I pray you, *Shrift*, mother of salvation,
     Help my good deeds for my piteous exclamation.
Confession.   I know your sorrow well, *Everyman*;
     Because with *Knowledge* ye come to me,
     I will you comfort as well as I can,
     And a precious jewel I will give thee,
     Called penance, wise voider of adversity;
     Therewith shall your body chastised be,
     With abstinence and perseverance in God's service:
     Here shall you receive that scourge of me,
     Which is penance strong, that ye must endure,
     To remember thy Saviour was scourged for thee
     With sharp scourges, and suffered it patiently;

34. *good conceit*] favorable opinion, i.e., highly esteemed by.

So must thou, or thou scape that painful pilgrimage;
Knowledge, keep him in this voyage,
And by that time *Good-Deeds* will be with thee.
But in any wise, be sure of mercy,
For your time draweth fast, and ye will saved be;
Ask God mercy, and He will grant truly,
When with the scourge of penance man doth him bind,
The oil of forgiveness then shall he find.

Everyman.   Thanked be God for his gracious work!
For now I will my penance begin;
This hath rejoiced and lighted my heart,
Though the knots be painful and hard within.

Knowledge.   *Everyman*, look your penance that ye fulfil,
What pain that ever it to you be,
And *Knowledge* shall give you counsel at will,
How your accounts ye shall make clearly.

Everyman.   O eternal God, O heavenly figure,
O way of rightwiseness, O goodly vision,
Which descended down in a virgin pure
Because he would *Everyman* redeem,
Which *Adam* forfeited by his disobedience:
O blessed Godhead, elect and high-divine,
Forgive my grievous offence;
Here I cry thee mercy in this presence.
O ghostly treasure, O ransomer and redeemer
Of all the world, hope and conductor,
Mirror of joy, and founder of mercy,
Which illumineth heaven and earth thereby,
Hear my clamorous complaint, though it late be;
Receive my prayers; unworthy in this heavy life,
Though I be, a sinner most abominable,
Yet let my name be written in *Moses'* table;
O *Mary*, pray to the Maker of all thing,
Me for to help at my ending,
And save me from the power of my enemy,
For *Death* assaileth me strongly;
And, Lady, that I may by means of thy prayer
Of your Son's glory to be partaker,
By the means of his passion I it crave,
I beseech you, help my soul to save. —
Knowledge, give me the scourge of penance;
My flesh therewith shall give a quittance:
I will now begin, if God give me grace.

Knowledge.   *Everyman*, God give you time and space:
        Thus I bequeath you in the hands of our Saviour,
        Thus may you make your reckoning sure.
Everyman.   In the name of the Holy Trinity,
        My body sore[35] punished shall be:
        Take this body for the sin of the flesh;
        Also thou delightest to go gay and fresh,
        And in the way of damnation thou did me bring;
        Therefore suffer now strokes and punishing.
        Now of penance I will wade the water clear,
        To save me from purgatory, that sharp fire.
Good-Deeds.   I thank God, now I can walk and go;
        And am delivered of my sickness and woe.
        Therefore with *Everyman* I will go, and not spare;
        His good works I will help him to declare.
Knowledge.   Now, *Everyman*, be merry and glad;
        Your *Good-Deeds* cometh now; ye may not be sad;
        Now is your *Good-Deeds* whole and sound,
        Going upright upon the ground.
Everyman.   My heart is light, and shall be evermore;
        Now will I smite faster than I did before.
Good-Deeds.   *Everyman*, pilgrim, my special friend,
        Blessed be thou without end;
        For thee is prepared the eternal glory.
        Ye have me made whole and sound,
        Therefore I will bide by thee in every stound.[36]
Everyman.   Welcome, my *Good-Deeds*; now I hear thy voice,
        I weep for very sweetness of love.
Knowledge.   Be no more sad, but ever rejoice,
        God seeth thy living in his throne above;
        Put on this garment to thy behove,[37]
        Which is wet with your tears,
        Or else before God you may it miss,
        When you to your journey's end come shall.
Everyman.   Gentle *Knowledge*, what do you it call?
Knowledge.   It is a garment of sorrow:
        From pain it will you borrow;
        Contrition it is,
        That getteth forgiveness;
        It pleaseth God passing well.

35. *sore*] grievously.
36. *stound*] season.
37. *behove*] advantage.

Good-Deeds.   *Everyman*, will you wear it for your heal?
Everyman.   Now blessed be *Jesu, Mary's* Son!
     For now have I on true contrition.
     And let us go now without tarrying;
     Good-Deeds, have we clear our reckoning?
Good-Deeds.   Yea, indeed I have it here.
Everyman.   Then I trust we need not fear;
     Now, friends, let us not part in twain.[38]
Knowledge.   Nay, Everyman, that will we not, certain.
Good-Deeds.   Yet must thou lead with thee
     Three persons of great might.
Everyman.   Who should they be?
Good-Deeds.   *Discretion* and *Strength* they hight,[39]
     And thy *Beauty* may not abide behind.
Knowledge.   Also ye must call to mind
     Your *Five-wits* as for your counsellors.
Good-Deeds.   You must have them ready at all hours.
Everyman.   How shall I get them hither?
Knowledge.   You must call them all together,
     And they will hear you incontinent.[40]
Everyman.   My friends, come hither and be present
     Discretion, Strength, my *Five-wits*, and *Beauty*.
Beauty.   Here at your will we be all ready.
     What will ye that we should do?
Good-Deeds.   That ye would with *Everyman* go,
     And help him in his pilgrimage,
     Advise you, will ye with him or not in that voyage?
Strength.   We will bring him all thither,
     To his help and comfort, ye may believe me.
Discretion.   So will we go with him all together.
Everyman.   Almighty God, loved thou be,
     I give thee laud that I have hither brought
     Strength, Discretion, Beauty, and *Five-wits*; lack I nought;
     And my *Good-Deeds*, with *Knowledge* clear,
     All be in my company at my will here;
     I desire no more to my business.
Strength.   And I, *Strength*, will by you stand in distress,
     Though thou would in battle fight on the ground.

38. *twain*] two.
39. *hight*] are called, named.
40. *incontinent*] immediately.

Five-wits.   And though it were through the world round,
   We will not depart for sweet nor sour.
Beauty.   No more will I unto death's hour,
   Whatsoever thereof befall.
Discretion.   *Everyman*, advise you first of all;
   Go with a good advisement and deliberation;
   We all give you virtuous monition[41]
   That all shall be well.
Everyman.   My friends, hearken what I will tell:
   I pray God reward you in his heavenly sphere.
   Now hearken, all that be here,
   For I will make my testament
   Here before you all present.
   In alms half my good I will give with my hands twain
   In the way of charity, with good intent,
   And the other half still shall remain
   In quiet to be returned there it ought to be.
   This I do in despite of the fiend of hell
   To go quite out of his peril
   Ever after and this day.
Knowledge.   *Everyman*, hearken what I say;
   Go to priesthood, I you advise,
   And receive of him in any wise
   The holy sacrament and ointment together;
   Then shortly see ye turn again hither;
   We will all abide you here.
Five-Wits.   Yea, *Everyman*, hie you that ye ready were,
   There is no emperor, king, duke, ne baron,
   That of God hath commission,
   As hath the least priest in the world being;
   For of the blessed sacraments pure and benign,
   He beareth the keys and thereof hath the cure
   For man's redemption, it is ever sure;
   Which God for our soul's medicine
   Gave us out of his heart with great pine;
   Here in this transitory life, for thee and me
   The blessed sacraments seven there be,
   Baptism, confirmation, with priesthood good,
   And the sacrament of God's precious flesh and blood,
   Marriage, the holy extreme unction, and penance;

41. *monition*] warning.

These seven be good to have in remembrance,
   Gracious sacraments of high divinity.
Everyman.   Fain would I receive that holy body
   And meekly to my ghostly father I will go.
Five-wits.   *Everyman,* that is the best that ye can do:
   God will you to salvation bring,
   For priesthood exceedeth all other thing;
   To us Holy Scripture they do teach,
   And converteth man from sin heaven to reach;
   God hath to them more power given,
   Than to any angel that is in heaven;
   With five words he may consecrate
   God's body in flesh and blood to make,
   And handleth his maker between his hands;
   The priest bindeth and unbindeth all bands,
   Both in earth and in heaven;
   Thou ministers all the sacraments seven;
   Though we kissed thy feet thou were worthy;
   Thou art surgeon that cureth sin deadly:
   No remedy we find under God
   But all only priesthood.
   Everyman, God gave priests that dignity,
   And setteth them in his stead among us to be;
   Thus be they above angels in degree.
Knowledge.   If priests be good it is so surely;
   But when Jesus hanged on the cross with great smart
   There he gave, out of his blessed heart,
   The same sacrament in great torment:
   He sold them not to us, that Lord Omnipotent.
   Therefore Saint Peter the apostle doth say
   That Jesu's curse hath all they
   Which God their Saviour do buy or sell,
   Or they for any money do take or tell.
   Sinful priests giveth the sinners example bad;
   Their children sitteth by other men's fires, I have heard;
   And some haunteth women's company,
   With unclean life, as lusts of lechery:
   These be with sin made blind.
Five-wits.   I trust to God no such may we find;
   Therefore let us priesthood honour,
   And follow their doctrine for our souls' succour;
   We be their sheep, and they shepherds be
   By whom we all be kept in surety.

Peace, for yonder I see *Everyman* come,
Which hath made true satisfaction.
Good-Deeds.   Methinketh it is he indeed.
Everyman.   Now Jesu be our alder speed.[42]
I have received the sacrament for my redemption,
And then mine extreme unction:
Blessed be all they that counselled me to take it!
And now, friends, let us go without longer respite;
I thank God that ye have tarried so long.
Now set each of you on this rod your hand,
And shortly follow me:
I go before, there I would be; God be our guide.
Strength.   *Everyman*, we will not from you go,
Till ye have gone this voyage long.
Discretion.   I, *Discretion*, will bide by you also.
Knowledge.   And though this pilgrimage be never so strong,
I will never part you fro:
Everyman, I will be as sure by thee
As ever I did by Judas Maccabee.
Everyman.   Alas, I am so faint I may not stand,
My limbs under me do fold;
Friends, let us not turn again to this land,
Not for all the world's gold,
For into this cave must I creep
And turn to the earth and there to sleep.
Beauty.   What, into this grave? alas!
Everyman.   Yea, there shall you consume[43] more and less.
Beauty.   And what, should I smother here?
Everyman.   Yea, by my faith, and never more appear.
In this world live no more we shall,
But in heaven before the highest Lord of all.
Beauty.   I cross out all this; adieu by Saint *John*;
I take my cap in my lap and am gone.
Everyman.   What, *Beauty*, whither will ye?
Beauty.   Peace, I am deaf; I look not behind me,
Not and thou would give me all the gold in thy chest.
Everyman.   Alas, whereto may I trust?
Beauty goeth fast away hie;
She promised with me to live and die.

42. *Now . . . speed.*] May Jesus be the helper of all.
43. *consume*] decay.

Strength.   *Everyman*, I will thee also forsake and deny;
 Thy game liketh me not at all.
Everyman.   Why, then ye will forsake me all.
 Sweet *Strength*, tarry a little space.
Strength.   Nay, sir, by the rood[44] of grace
 I will hie me from thee fast,
 Though thou weep till thy heart brast.[45]
Everyman.   Ye would ever bide by me, ye said.
Strength.   Yea, I have you far enough conveyed;
 Ye be old enough, I understand,
 Your pilgrimage to take on hand;
 I repent me that I hither came.
Everyman.   *Strength*, you to displease I am to blame;
 Will you break promise that is debt?
Strength.   In faith, I care not;
 Thou art but a fool to complain,
 You spend your speech and waste your brain;
 Go thrust thee into the ground.
Everyman.   I had wend surer I should you have found.
 He that trusteth in his *Strength*
 She him deceiveth at the length.
 Both *Strength* and *Beauty* forsaketh me,
 Yet they promised me fair and lovingly.
Discretion.   *Everyman*, I will after *Strength* be gone,
 As for me I will leave you alone.
Everyman.   Why, *Discretion*, will ye forsake me?
Discretion.   Yea, in faith, I will go from thee,
 For when *Strength* goeth before
 I follow after evermore.
Everyman.   Yet, I pray thee, for the love of the Trinity,
 Look in my grave once piteously.
Discretion.   Nay, so nigh will I not come.
 Farewell, every one!
Everyman.   O all thing faileth, save God alone;
 Beauty, *Strength*, and *Discretion*;
 For when *Death* bloweth his blast,
 They all run from me full fast.
Five-wits.   *Everyman*, my leave now of thee I take;
 I will follow the other, for here I thee forsake.

44. *rood*] cross.
45. *brast*] break.

Everyman.   Alas! then may I wail and weep,
    For I took you for my best friend.
Five-wits.   I will no longer thee keep;
    Now farewell, and there an end.
Everyman.   O Jesu, help, all hath forsaken me!
Good-Deeds.   Nay, *Everyman*, I will bide with thee,
    I will not forsake thee indeed;
    Thou shalt find me a good friend at need.
Everyman.   Gramercy, *Good-Deeds*; now may I true friends see;
    They have forsaken me every one;
    I loved them better than my *Good-Deeds* alone.
    Knowledge, will ye forsake me also?
Knowledge.   Yea, *Everyman*, when ye to death do go:
    But not yet for no manner of danger.
Everyman.   Gramercy, *Knowledge*, with all my heart.
Knowledge.   Nay, yet I will not from hence depart,
    Till I see where ye shall be come.
Everyman.   Methinketh, alas, that I must be gone,
    To make my reckoning and my debts pay,
    For I see my time is nigh spent away.
    Take example, all ye that this do hear or see,
    How they that I loved best do forsake me,
    Except my *Good-Deeds* that bideth truly.
Good-Deeds.   All earthly things is but vanity:
    Beauty, *Strength*, and *Discretion*, do man forsake,
    Foolish friends and kinsmen, that fair spake,
    All fleeth save *Good-Deeds*, and that am I.
Everyman.   Have mercy on me, God most mighty;
    And stand by me, thou Mother and Maid, holy *Mary*.
Good-Deeds.   Fear not, I will speak for thee.
Everyman.   Here I cry God mercy.
Good-Deeds.   Short our end, and minish[46] our pain;
    Let us go and never come again.
Everyman.   Into thy hands, Lord, my soul I commend;
    Receive it, Lord, that it be not lost;
    As thou me boughtest, so me defend,
    And save me from the fiend's boast,
    That I may appear with that blessed host
    That shall be saved at the day of doom.

46. *minish*] diminish.

In manus tuas[47] — of might's most
For ever — *commendo spiritum meum.*[48]
Knowledge.   Now hath he suffered that we all shall endure;
The *Good-Deeds* shall make all sure.
Now hath he made ending;
Methinketh that I hear angels sing
And make great joy and melody,
Where *Everyman's* soul received shall be.
Angel.   Come, excellent elect spouse to Jesu:
Hereabove thou shalt go
Because of thy singular virtue:
Now the soul is taken the body fro;
Thy reckoning is crystal-clear.
Now shalt thou into the heavenly sphere,
Unto the which all ye shall come
That liveth well before the day of doom.
Doctor.   This moral men may have in mind;
Ye hearers, take it of worth, old and young,
And forsake pride, for he deceiveth you in the end,
And remember *Beauty, Five-wits, Strength*, and *Discretion*,
They all at the last do *Everyman* forsake,
Save his *Good-Deeds*, there doth he take.
But beware, and they be small
Before God, he hath no help at all.
None excuse may be there for *Everyman*:
Alas, how shall he do then?
For after death amends may no man make,
For then mercy and pity do him forsake.
If his reckoning be not clear when he do come,
God will say — *ite maledicti in ignem æternum.*[49]
And he that hath his account whole and sound,
High in heaven he shall be crowned;
Unto which place God bring us all thither
That we may live body and soul together.
Thereto help the Trinity,
Amen, say ye, for saint *Charity.*

THUS ENDETH THIS MORALL PLAY OF EVERYMAN.

---

47. *In manus tuas*] "Into thy hands."
48. *commendo spiritum meum.*] I commend my spirit.
49. *ite . . . æternum*] "Depart, ye cursed, into everlasting fire" (Matthew 25:41).

HICKSCORNER

Characters

Pity	Contemplation
Perseverance	Freewill
Imagination	Hickscorner

[*Pity and Contemplation.*]

Pity.   Now Jesu the gentle, that brought Adam fro hell,
Save you all, sovereigns, and solace you send:
And, of this matter that I begin to tell,
I pray you of audience, till I have made an end;
For I say to you, my name is Pity,
That ever yet hath been man's friend.
In the bosom of the second person in Trinity[1]
I sprang as a plant, man's miss to amend;
You for to help I put to my hand:
Record I take of Mary that wept tears of blood;
I Pity within her heart did stand;
When she saw her son on the rood,[2]
The sword of sorrow gave that lady wound;
When a spear clave her son's heart asunder,
She cried out, and fell to the ground;
Though she was woe, it was little wonder,
This delicate colour [had] that goodly lady,
Full pale and wan, she saw her son all dead,
Splayed on a cross with the five wells of pity,[3]

---

1. *second . . . Trinity*] The Holy Trinity is the Father, the Son and the Holy Ghost, so the reference here is to Christ.
2. *rood*] cross.
3. *five wells of pity*] the five wounds received by Christ on the cross from the nails in His hands and feet and from the spear thrust in His side.

Of purple velvet powdered with roses red.
Lo, I Pity thus made your errand to be sped,
Or else man for ever should have been forlore.
A maiden so laid his life to wed,
Crowned as a king the thorns pricked him sore.
Charity and I of true love leads the double rein;
Whoso me loveth damned never shall be.
Of some virtuous company I would be fain;[4]
For all that will to heaven needs must come by me,
Chief porter I am in that heavenly city,
And now here will I rest me a little space,
Till it please Jesu of his grace
Some virtuous fellowship for to send.

Contemplation.   Christ that was christened, crucified, and crowned,
In his bosom true love was gaged[5] with a spear,
His veins brast[6] and bruised, and to a pillar bound,
With scourges he was lashed, the knots the skin tare,[7]
On his neck to Calvary the great cross he bare,
His blood ran to the ground, as Scripture doth tell:
His burden was so heavy, that down under it he fell,
Lo, I am kin to the Lord, which is God's son;
My name is written foremost in the book of life,
For I am perfect Contemplation,
And brother to holy church that is our Lord's wife.
John Baptist, Anthony, and Jerome, with many mo,
Followed me here in holt,[8] heath, and in wilderness;
I ever with them went where they did go,
Night and day toward the way of rightwiseness:
I am the chief lantern of all holiness,
Of prelates and priests I am their patron;
No armour so strong in no distress,
Habergeon, helm, ne yet no Jeltron,
To fight with Satan am I the champion,[9]
That dare abide, and manfully stand:
Fiends flee away, where they see me come;
But I will show you why I came to this land

4. *fain*] pleased.
5. *gaged*] gauged, measured.
6. *brast*] burst.
7. *tare*] tore.
8. *holt*] woods.
9. *No armour . . . champion*] No armour —neither habergeon (jacket of mail), helm nor Jeltron (i.e., sheltron, or troops in close battle array) —is stronger than I in the fight against Satan.

For to preach and teach of God's sooth saws,[10]
Ayenst[11] vice that doth rebel ayenst him and his laws.·
Pity.   God speed! good brother; fro whence came you now?
Contemplation.   Sir, I came from Perseverance to seek you.
Pity.   Why, sir, know you me?
Contemplation.   Yea, sir, and have done long; your name is Pity.
Pity.   Your name fain would I know.
Contemplation.   Indeed I am called Contemplation,
    That useth to live solitarily;
    In woods and in wildness I walk alone,
    Because I would say my prayers devoutly;
    I love not with me to have much company:
    But Perseverance oft with me doth meet,
    When I think on thoughts that is full heavenly;
    Thus he and I together full sweetly doth sleep.
Pity.   I thank God that we be met together.
Contemplation.   Sir, I trust that Perseverance shortly will come hither.
Pity.   Then I think to hear some good tiding.
Contemplation.   I warrant you, brother, that he is coming.

[*Enter Perseverance.*]

Perseverance.   The eternal God, that named was Messias,
    He give you grace to come to his glory,
    Wherever is joy in the celestial place,
    When you of Satan winneth the victory,
    Everyman ought to be glad to have in company,
    For I am named good Perseverance,
    That ever is guided by virtuous governance;
    I am never variable, but doth continue,
    Still going upward the ladder of grace,
    And lode[12] in me planted is so true,
    And from the poor man I will never turn my face:
    When I go by myself oft I do remember
    The great kindness that God showed unto man,
    For to be born in the month of December,
    When the day waxeth short, and the night long,
    Of his goodness that champion strong
    Descended down fro the Father of rightwiseness,
    And rested in Mary the flower of meekness.

10. *sooth saws*] true sayings.
11. *Ayenst*] Against.
12. *lode*] guidance.

Now to this place hither come I am
To seek Contemplation my kinsman.
Contemplation.   What, brother Perseverance! ye be welcome.
Perseverance.   And so be you also, Contemplation.
Contemplation.   Lo, here is our master Pity.
Perseverance.   Now truly ye be welcome into this country.
Pity.   I thank ye heartily, sir Perseverance.
Perseverance.   Master Pity, one thing is come to my remembrance;
    What tithings hear you now?
Pity.   Sir, such as I can I shall show you:
    I have heard many men complain piteously;
    They say they be smitten with the swerd[13] of poverty,
    In every place where I do go:
    Few friends poverty doth find,
    And these rich men been unkind;
    For their neighbours they will nought do,
    Widows doth curse lords and gentle men,
    For they constrain them to marry with their men,
    Yea, whether they will or no:
    Men marry for good,[14] and that is damnable,
    Yea, with old women that is fifty and beyond:
    The peril now no man dread will;
    All is not God's law that is used in land;
    Beware will they not, till death in his hand
    Taketh his sword, and smiteth asunder the life vein,
    And with his mortal stroke cleaveth the heart atwain:[15]
    They trust so in mercy, the lantern of brightness,
    That no thing do they dread God's rightwiseness.
Perseverance.   O Jesu, sir! here is a heavy tiding.
Pity.   Sir, this is true, that I do bring.
Contemplation.   How am I beloved, master Pity, where ye come?
Pity.   In good faith, people have now small devotion;
    And as for with you, brother Contemplation,
    There meddleth few or none.
Contemplation.   Yet, I trust, that priests love me well?
Pity.   But a few, i-wis,[16] and some never a deal.
Contemplation.   Why, sir, without me they may not live clean.

13. *swerd*] sword.
14. *for good*] for worldly goods, gain.
15. *atwain*] in two.
16. *i-wis*] certainly, truly.

Pity.   Nay, that is the least thought that they have of fifteen;
    And that maketh me full heavy.
Contemplation.   How, trow[17] ye that there be no remedy?
Pity.   Full hard, for sin is now so grievous and ill,
    That I think that it be growen[18] to an impossible,
    And yet one thing maketh me ever mourning:
    That priests lack utterance to show their cunning;
    And all the while that clerks do use so great sin,
    Among the lay people look never for no mending.
Perseverance.   Alas! that is a heavy case,
    That so great sin is used in every place:
    I pray God it amend.
Contemplation.   Now God, that ever hath been man's friend,
    Some better tidings soon us send!
    For now I must be gone.
    Farewell! good brethren here;
    A great errand I have elsewhere,
    That must needs be done:
    I trust I will not long tarry;
    Thither will I hie[19] me shortly,
    And come again when I have done.
Perseverance.   Hither again, I trust, you will come;
    Therefore, God be with you!
Contemplation.   Sir, needs I must depart now;
    Jesu, me speed this day!
Perseverance.   Now, brother Contemplation, let us go our way.

[*Exit Contemplation and Perseverance: enter Freewill.*]

Freewill.   Aware, fellows! and stand a-room![20]
    How say you? Am not I a goodly person?
    I trow you know not such a guest.
    What, sirs! I tell you my name is Freewill;
    I may choose whether I do good or ill;
    But, for all that, I will do as me list.[21]
    My conditions ye know not, perde! — [22]
    I can fight, chide, and be merry;
    Full soon of my company ye would be weary

17. *trow*] believe, hope.
18. *growen*] grown.
19. *hie*] hasten, hurry.
20. *a-room*] aside.
21. *list*] please, wish.
22. *perde*] corruption of *par Dieu* (by God); a mild oath.

And[23] ye knew all.
What! fill the cup, and make good cheer!
I trow I have a noble[24] here:
Who lent it me? By Christ! a frere;[25]
And I gave him a fall.
Where be ye, sir? be ye at home?
Cock's passion![26] my noble is turned to a stone.[27]
Where lay I last? Beshrew your heart, John;
Now, by these bones, she hath beguiled me:
Let see; a penny my supper, a piece of flesh tenpence;
My bed right nought: let all this expense —
Now, by these bones, I have lost a halfpenny.
Who lay there? my fellow Imagination;
He and I had good communication
Of Sir John and Sybil,
How they were spied in bed together;
And he prayed her oft to come hither,
For to sing *lo, le, lo, lowe.*
They twain together had good sport;
But at the stews' side I lost a groat:[28]
I trow I shall never i-the.[29]
My fellow promised me here to meet,
But I trow the whoreson be asleep
With a wench somewhere.
How, Imagination, come hither,
And you thrive, I lose a feather;
Beshrew your heart, appear.

[*Enter Imagination.*]

Imagination.   What, how, how, who called after me?
Freewill.   Come near, ye shall never i-the,
      Where have ye be so long?
Imagination.   By God! with me it is all wrong,
      I have a pair of sore buttocks,

---

23. *And*] As used here, "if."
24. *noble*] gold coin.
25. *frere*] friar.
26. *Cock's passion!*] Christ's passion (on the cross), an oath; "Cock's" is also used preceding "bones" and "body" in other oaths throughout the play.
27. *Where . . . a stone*] Freewill is addressing the coin, which he has lost. He finds a stone in its place.
28. *stews' . . . groat*] a stew was the word for both a brothel and a prostitute; a groat was a silver coin.
29. *i-the*] to thrive.

All in irons was my song,
Even now I sat gyved[30] in a pair of stocks.
Freewill.   Cock's passion! and how so?
Imagination.   Sir, I will tell you what I have do:
I met with a wench, and she was fair,
And of love heartily I did pray her,
And so promised her money:
Sir, she winked on me, and said nought,
But by her look I knew her thought;
Then into love's dance we were brought,
That we played the pyrdewy:[31]
I wot[32] not what we did together,
But a knave catchpole nighed us near,[33]
And so did us aspy;
A stripe he gave me, I fled my touch,
And from my girdle he plucked my pouch:
By your leave he left me never a penny:
Lo, nought have I but a buckle,
And yet I can imagine things subtle
For to get money plenty;
In Westminster Hall every term I am,
To me is kin many a great gentleman,
I am knowen in every country;
And I were dead, the lawyers' thrift[34] were lost:
For this will I do, if men would do cost,
Prove right wrong, and all by reason,
And make men lese[35] both house and land,
For all that they can do in a little season,
Peach[36] men of treason privily I can,
And when me list, to hang a true man.
If they will be money tell,
Thieves I can help out of prison,
And into lords' favours I can get me soon,
And be of their privy council.
But, Freewill, my dear brother,

---

30. *gyved*] fettered, shackled.
31. *pyrdewy*] exact meaning unclear, though it is obvious from context.
32. *wot*] know.
33. *catchpole ... near*] A sheriff's officer, especially one who makes arrest for bad debts (catchpole), approached (nighed) the two.
34. *thrift*] work, employment.
35. *lese*] lose.
36. *Peach*] Give incriminating evidence against.

Saw you nought of Hickscorner?
He promised me to come hither.
Freewill.   Why, sir, knowest thou him?
Imagination.   Yea, yea, man; he is full nigh of my kin,
  And in Newgate[37] we dwelled together;
For he and I were both shackled in a fetter.
Freewill.   Sir, lay you beneath or on high on the seller?[38]
Imagination.   Nay, i-wis, among the thickest of yeomen of the collar.[39]
Freewill.   By God! then you were in great fear.
Imagination.   Sir, had I not been, two hundred had been thrust in an
    halter.
Freewill.   And what life have they there, all that great sort?
Imagination.   By God, sir! once a year some taw halts[40] of Burpost:
  Yea, at Tyburn[41] there standeth the great frame,
  And some take a fall that maketh their neck lame.
Freewill.   Yea, but can they then go no more?
Imagination.   Oh, no, man; the wrest[42] is twist so sore,[43]
  For as soon as they have said *In manus tuas*[44] once,
  By God, their breath is stopped at once.
Freewill.   Why, do they pray in that place there?
Imagination.   Yea, sir, they stand in great fear,
  And so fast tangled in that snare,
  It falleth to their lot to have the same share.
Freewill.   That is a knavish sight to see them totter on a beam.
Imagination.   Sir, the whoresons could not convey clean;[45]
  For, and they could have carried by craft as I can,
  In process of years each of them should be a gentleman.
  Yet as for me I was never thief;
  If my hands were smitten off, I can steal with my teeth;
  For ye know well, there is craft in daubing:[46]
  I can look in a man's face and pick his purse,

37. *Newgate*] the famous London prison; the first structure was built in 1422 and the last in
    1770–78; it was razed in 1902.
38. *seller*] cellar, prison cell.
39. *yeomen of the collar*] prisoners destined for the hangman's noose.
40. *taw halts*] possibly, "taw" is a form of "tow," or rope, and halts is perhaps short for halter
    or noose.
41. *Tyburn*] a public place of execution in London; "great frame" refers to the gallows
    there.
42. *the wrest*] the wrench.
43. *sore*] severely, violently.
44. *In manus tuas*] Literally, "Into thy hands," a prayer by the dying, committing their soul
    to God's care.
45. *convey clean*] steal (convey) without getting caught.
46. *daubing*] to cover up by deceit.

And tell new tidings that was never true, i-wis,
For my hood is all lined with lesing.
Freewill.   Yea, but went ye never to Tyburn a pilgrimage?
Imagination.   No, i-wis; nor none of my lineage,
For we be clerks all, and can our neck verse,
And with an ointment the judge's hand I can grease,
That will heal sores that be incurable.
Freewill.   Why, were ye never found reprovable?
Imagination.   Yes, once I stall[47] a horse in the field,
And leapt on him for to have ridden my way:
At the last a baily[48] me met and beheld,
And bad me stand; then was I in a fray:
He asked, whither with that horse I would gone;
And then I told him it was mine own:
He said I had stolen him; and I said nay:
This is, said he, my brother's hackney.
For, and I had not excused me, without fail,
By our lady, he would have lad me straight to jail;
And then I told him the horse was like mine,
A brown bay, a long mane, and did halt behine,[49]
Thus I told him, that such another horse I did lack;
And yet I never saw him, nor came on his back:
So I delivered him the horse again.
And when he was gone, then was I fain:
For and I had not excused me the better,
I know well I should have danced in a fetter.
Freewill.   And said he no more to thee but so?
Imagination.   Yea, he pretended[50] me much harm to do;
But I told him that morning was a great mist,
That what horse it was I ne wist:[51]
Also I said, that in my head I had the megrin,[52]
That made me dazzle so in mine eyen,
That I might not well see.
And thus he departed shortly from me.
Freewill.   Yea, but where is Hickscorner now?
Imagination.   Some of these young men hath hid him in

---

47. *stall*] stole.
48. *baily*] bailiff, officer of the law.
49. *behine*] behind.
50. *pretended*] intended.
51. *I ne wist*] I did not know.
52. *megrin*] migraine headache.

Their bosoms, I warrant ye:
Let us make a cry, that he may us hear.
Freewill.   How now, Hickscorner, appear;
I trow thou be hid in some corner.

[*Enter Hickscorner.*]

Hickscorner.   Ale[53] the helm, ale, veer, shoot off, veer sail, veer-a.
Freewill.   Cock's body! hark! he is a ship on the sea.
Hickscorner.   God speed, God speed! who called after me?
Imagination.   What, brother, welcome by this precious body;
I am glad that I you see,
It was told me that you were hanged;
But out of what country come ye?
Hickscorner.   Sirs, I have been in many a country;
As in France, Ireland, and in Spain,
Portingal, Sevile, also in Almaine;
Friesland, Flanders, and in Burgoine,
Calabria, Pugle, and Erragon,
Britain, Biske, and also in Gascoine,
Naples, Greece, and in middes[54] of Scotland;
At Cape Saint Vincent, and in the new found island,
I have been in Gene and in Cowe,
Also in the land of Rumbelow,[55]
Three mile out of hell;
At Rhodes, Constantine, and in Babylon,
In Cornwall, and in Northumberland,
Where men seethe rushes in gruel;
Yea, sir, in Chaldæa, Tartary, and India,
And in the Land of Women, that few men doth find:
In all these countries have I be.
Freewill.   Sir, what tidings hear ye now on the sea?
Hickscorner.   We met of ships a great navy,
Full of people that would into Ireland;
And they came out of this country:
They will never more come to England.
Imagination.   Whence were the ships of them? knowest thou none?
Hickscorner.   Harken, and I will show you their names each one:
First was the *Regent*, with the *Michael* of Brikilse;
The *George*, with the *Gabriel*, and the *Anne* of Fowey;

53. *Ale*] a-lee; to the windward.
54. *middes*] midst.
55. *Rumbelow*] fictional land from an ancient sailing song.

The *Star* of Saltash, with the *Jesus* of Plymouth;
Also the *Hermitage*, with the *Barbara* of Dartmouth,
The *Nicolas* and the *Mary Bellouse* of Bristow,
With the *Ellen* of London and *James* also:
Great was the people that was in them,
All true religious and holy women:
There was Truth and his kinsmen,
With Patience, Meekness, and Humility,
And all true maidens with their virginity,
Royal preachers, sadness and charity,
Right conscience and faith, with devotion,
And all true monks that keep their religion,
True buyers and sellers, and alms-deed doers,
Piteous people, that be of sin destroyers,
With just abstinence, and good councillors,
Mourners for sin, with lamentation,
And good rich men that helpeth folk out of prison,
True wedlock was there also,
With young men that ever in prayer did go,
The ships were laden with such unhappy company,
But at the last God shope[56] a remedy,
For they all in the sea were drowned,
And on a quicksand they strake[57] to ground;
The sea swallowed them everychone,
I wot well alive there scaped none.

Imagination.   Lo, now my heart is glad and merry;
For joy now let us sing "Derry, derry."

Hickscorner.   Fellows, they shall never more us withstand;
For I see them all drowned in the Rase[58] of Ireland.

Freewill.   Yea, but yet hark, Hickscorner,
What company was in your ship, that came over?

Hickscorner.   Sir, I will aid you to understand,
There were good fellows above five thousand,
And all they been kin to us three:
There was falsehood, favell,[59] and jollity,
Yea, thieves, and whores, with other good company,
Liars, backbiters, and flatterers the while,
Brawlers, liars, jetters, and chiders,

---

56. *shope*] shaped, made, created.
57. *strake*] struck.
58. *Rase*] Now spelled "Race," a strong current in the sea or river.
59. *favell*] flattery, cajolery.

Walkers by night, with great murderers,
Overthwart guile[rs] and jolly carders,
Oppressors of people, with many swearers;
There was false law with horrible vengeance,
Froward obstination with mischievous governance,
Wanton wenches, and also michers,[60]
With many other of the devil's officers;
And hatred, that is so mighty and strong,
Hath made a vow for ever to dwell in England.

Imagination.   But is that true, that thou dost show now?

Hickscorner.   Sir, every word as I do tell you.

Freewill.   Of whence is your ship? of London?

Hickscorner.   Yea, i-wis from thence did she come;
And she is named *The Envy*,
I tell you, a great vessel and a mighty:
The owner of her is called Ill-Will,
Brother to Jack Poller of Shooter's Hill.[61]

Imagination.   Sir, what office in the ship bare ye?

Hickscorner.   Marry! I kept a fair shop of bawdry,
I had three wenches that were full praty,[62]
Jane true and thriftless, and wanton Sybil,
If you ride her a journey, she will make you weary,
For she is trusty at need:
If ye will hire her for your pleasure,
I warrant, tire her shall ye never,
She is so sure in deed;
Ride, and you will, ten times a-day,
I warrant you she will never say nay,
My life I dare lay to wed.

Imagination.   Now pluck up your hearts, and make good cheer;
These tidings liketh me wonder well,
Now virtue shall draw arear arear:
Hark, fellows! a good sport I can you tell,
At the stews we will lie to-night,
And by my troth, if all go right,
I will beguile some praty wench,
To get me money at a pinch.
How say you? shall we go thither?

60. *michers*] truants, petty thieves.
61. *Jack Poller of Shooter's Hill*] Jack Poller is a generic term for a robber ("polled" meant plundered or stripped); Shooter's Hill was near Greenwich, then an outlying area of London rife with thieves.
62. *praty*] pretty.

Let us keep company altogether,
And I would that we had God's curse,
If we somewhere do not get a purse;
Every man bear his dagger naked in his hand,
And if we meet a true man, make him stand,
Or else that he bear a stripe;[63]
If that he struggle, and make any work,
Lightly strike him to the heart,
And throw him into Thames quite.

Freewill.   Nay, three knaves in a leash is good at nale:[64]
But thou lubber Imagination,
That cuckold thy father, where is he become?
At Newgate doth he lie still at jail?

Imagination.   Avaunt, whoreson! thou shalt bear me a stripe;
Say'st thou, that my mother was a whore?

Freewill.   Nay, sir, but the last night
I saw Sir John and she tumbled on the floor.

Imagination.   Now, by Cock's heart! thou shalt lose an arm.

Hickscorner.   Nay, sir, I charge you do him no harm.

Imagination.   And thou make too much, I will break thy head too.

Hickscorner.   By Saint Mary! and I wist that, I would be ago.

Imagination.   Aware, aware! the whoreson shall aby,[65]
His priest will I be, by Cock's body!

Hickscorner.   Keep peace, lest knaves' blood be shed.

Freewill.   By God! if his was nought, mine was as bad.

Imagination.   By Cock's heart! he shall die on this dagger.

Hickscorner.   By our Lady! then will ye be strangled in a halter.

Imagination.   The whoreson shall eat him, as far as he shall wade.

Hickscorner.   Beshrew your heart! and put up your blade,
Sheathe your whittle,[66] or by Jis![67] that was never born,
I will rap you on the costard[68] with my horn;
What, will ye play all the knave?

Imagination.   By Cock's heart! and thou a buffet shalt have.

Freewill.   Lo, sirs! here is a fair company, God us save!
For if any of us three be mayor of London,
I-wis, i-wis, I will ride to Rome on my thumb:

63. *stripe*] weal or welt caused by a damaging blow.
64. *at nale*] at the alehouse.
65. *aby*] pay the penalty for, suffer.
66. *whittle*] dagger.
67. *Jis*] Jesus.
68. *costard*] head.

Alas! ah, see; is not this a great feres?[69]
I would they were in a mill-pool above the ears;
And then I durst warrant, they would depart anon.
Hickscorner.   Help, help! for the passion of my soul;
He hath made a great hole in my poll,[70]
That all my wit is set to the ground:
Alas! a leech[71] for to help my wound.
Imagination.   Nay, i-wis, whoreson, I will bite thee, ere I go.
Freewill.   Alas! good sir, what have I do?
Imagination.   Ware,[72] make room! he shall have a stripe, I trow.

[*Enter Pity.*]

Pity.   Peace, peace, sirs, I command you!
Imagination.   Avaunt, old churl! whence comest thou?
And thou make too much, I shall break thy brow,
And send thee home again.
Pity.   Ah, good sir, the peace I would have kept fain;
Mine office is to see no man slain;
And where they do amiss, to give them good counsel,
Sin to forsake, and God's law them tell.
Imagination.   Ah, sir! I ween'd[73] thou hadst been drowned and gone:
But I have spied, that there scaped one.
Hickscorner.   Imagination, do by the counsel of me,
Be agreed with Freewill, and let us good fellows be;
And then, as for this churl Pity,
Shall curse the time that ever he came to land.
Imagination.   Brother Freewill, give me your hand,
And all mine ill will I forgive thee.
Freewill.   Sir, I thank you heartily;
But what shall we do with this churl Pity?
Imagination.   I will go to him, and pick a quarrel,
And make him a thief, and say he did steal
Of mine forty pound in a bag.
Freewill.   By God! that tidings will make him sad;
And I will go fetch a pair of gyves,[74]
For in good faith he shall be set fast by the heels.

69. *feres*] company, i.e. group of friends, companions.
70. *poll*] head, skull.
71. *leech*] physician.
72. *Ware*] Beware.
73. *ween'd*] thought, believed, supposed.
74. *gyves*] leg-irons.

Hickscorner.   Have ado lightly, and be gone,
    And let us twain with him alone.
Freewill.   Now, farewell, I beshrew you everychone.[75]

[*Exit Freewill.*]

Hickscorner.   Ho, ho! Freewill you threw, and no mo.
Imagination.   Thou lewd fellow! say'st thou that thy name is Pity?
    Who sent thee hither to control me?
Pity.   Good sir, it is my property[76]
    For to despise sinful living,
    And unto virtue men to bring,
    If that they will do after me.
Imagination.   What, sir, art thou so pure holy?
    Ah, see, this caitiff would be praised, I trow;
    And you thrive this year, I will lose a penny.
    Lo, sirs! outward he beareth a fair face;
    But, and he meet with a wench in a privy place,
    I trow he would show her but little grace:
    By God! ye may trust me.
Hickscorner.   Lo! will ye not see this caitiff's meaning?
    He would destroy us all, and all our kin,
    Yet had I liever[77] see him hanged by the chin,
    Rather than that should be brought about;
    And with this dagger thou shalt have a clout,
    Without thou wilt be lightly be gone.
Imagination.   Nay, brother, lay hand on him soon;
    For he japed[78] my wife, and made me cuckold,
    And yet the traitor was so bold,
    That he stale forty pound of mine in money.
Hickscorner.   By Saint Mary! then he shall not scape;
    We will lead him straight to Newgate,
    For ever there shall he lie.

[*Freewill returns.*]

Freewill.   Ah, see, ah, see, sirs! what I have brought,
    A medicine for a pair of sore shins;
    At the King's Bench, sirs, I have you sought,
    But I pray you, who shall wear these?
Hickscorner.   By God! this fellow that may not go hence,

75. *everychone*] everyone.
76. *property*] trait peculiar to an individual; virtue.
77. *liever*] rather, prefer.
78. *japed*] had sexual intercourse with.

I will go give him these hose rings;[79]
Now, i-faith, they be worth forty pence,
But to his hands I lack two bonds.
Imagination.   Hold, whoreson! here is an halter;
Bind him fast, and make him sure.

[*They bind Pity.*]

Pity.   O men, let truth, that is the true man,
Be your guider, or else ye be forlorn;
Lay no false witness, as nigh as ye can,
On none; for afterward ye will repent it full sore.
Freewill.   Nay, nay, I care not therefore.
Hickscorner.   Yea, when my soul hangeth on the hedge-cast stones,
For I tell thee plainly by Cock's bones!
Thou shalt be guided, and laid in irons,
They fared even so.
Pity.   Well-a-way, sir, what have I do?
Imagination.   Well, well, that thou shalt know, ere thou go.
Pity.   O sirs, I see it cannot be amended,
You do me wrong, for I have not offended:
Remember God that is our heaven king,
For he will reward you after your deserving;
When death with his mace doth you arrest;
We all to him owe fea'ty[80] and service,
From the ladder of life down he will thee thrust,
Then mastership may not help, nor great office.
Freewill.   What, death, and he were here, he should sit by thee;
Trowest thou, that he be able to strive with us three?
Nay, nay, nay.
Imagination.   Well, fellows, now let us go our way;
For at Shooter's Hill we have a game to play.
Hickscorner.   In good faith, I will tarry no longer space.

[*Exit Imagination, Freewill, and Hickscorner.*]

Freewill.   Beshrew him for me, that is last out of this place.
Pity.   Lo, Lords, they may curse the time they were born,
For the weeds that overgroweth the corn,
They troubled me guiltless, and wote[81] not why,

79. *hose rings*] leg-shackles, fetters.
80. *fea'ty*] fealty; fidelity, loyalty.
81. *wote*] know.

For God's love yet will I suffer patiently:
We all may say well-a-way, for sin that is now-a-day.
Lo, virtue is vanished for ever and aye;
Worse was it never.
We have plenty of great oaths,
And cloth enough in our clothes,
But charity many men loathes,
Worse was it never.
Alas, now is lechery called love indeed,
And murder named manhood in every need,
Extortion is called law, so God me speed;
Worse was it never.
Youth walketh by night with swords and knives.
And ever among true men leseth their lives,
Like heretics we occupy other men's wives,
Now-a-days in England:
Bawds be the destroyers of many young women,
And full lewd counsel they give unto them;
How you do marry, beware, you young men,
The wise never tarrieth too long;
There be many great scorners,
But for sin there be few mourners;
We have but few true lovers
In no place now-a-days;
There be many goodly-gilt knaves,
And I know, as many apparelled wives,
Yet many of them be unthrifty of their lives,
And all set in pride to go gay.
Mayors on sin doeth no correction,
While gentle men beareth truth adown;
Avoutry[82] is suffered in every town,
Amendment is there none,
And God's commandments we break them all ten.
Devotion is gone many days sin.
Let us amend us, we true Christian men,
Ere death make you groan.
Courtiers go gay, and take little wages,
And many with harlots at the tavern haunts,
They be yeomen of the wreath[83] that be shackled in gyves;
On themselves they have no pity:

82. *Avoutry*] Adultery.
83. *yeomen of the wreath*] men destined to hang; cf. note 39.

God punisheth full sore with great sickness,
As pox, pestilence, purple,[84] and axes,
Some dieth suddenly that death full perilous,
Yet was there never so great poverty.
There be some sermons made by noble doctors;
But truly the fiend doth stop men's ears,
For God nor good man some people not fears;
Worse was it never.
All truth is not best said,
And our preachers now-a-days be half afraid:
When we do amend, God would be well apaid;
Worse was it never.

[*Enter Contemplation and Perseverance.*]

Contemplation. What, Master Pity, how is it with you?
Perseverance. Sir, we be sorry to see you in this case now.
Pity. Brethren, here were three perilous men,
    Freewill, Hickscorner, and Imagination;
    They said, I was a thief, and laid felony upon me,
    And bound me in irons, as ye may see.
Contemplation. Where be the traitors become now?
Pity. In good faith, I cannot show you.
Perseverance. Brother, let us unbind him of his bonds.
Contemplation. Unloose the feet and the hands.

[*They loose Pity.*]

Pity. I thank you for your great kindness,
    That you two show in this distress;
    For they were men without any mercy,
    That delighteth all in mischief and tyranny.
Perseverance. I think, they will come hither again,
    Freewill and Imagination, both twain:
    Them will I exhort to virtuous living,
    And unto virtue them to bring,
    By the help of you, Contemplation.
Contemplation. Do my counsel, brother Pity;
    Go you, and seek them through the country,
    In village, town, borough, and city,
    Throughout all the realm of England:
    When you them meet, lightly them arrest,
    And in prison put them fast,

84. *purple*] purple fever; a fever with an inflamed skin, especially in the face.

        Bind them sure in irons strong;
        For they be so fast and subtle;
        That they will you beguile,
        And do true men wrong.

Perseverance.   Brother Pity, do as he hath said,
        In every quarter look you espy,
        And let good watch for them be laid,
        In all the haste that thou can, and that privily;
        For, and they come hither, they shall not scape,
        For all the craft that they can make.

Pity.   Well, then will I hie me as fast as I may,
        And travel through every country;
        Good watch shall be laid in every way,
        That they steal not into sanctuary.
        Now farewell, brethren, and pray for me;
        For I must go hence in deed.

Perseverance.   Now God be your good speed!

Contemplation.   And ever you defend, when you have need.

Pity.   Now, brethren both, I thank you.

[*Exit Pity and enter Freewill.*]

Freewill.   Make you room for a gentleman, sirs, and peace;
        "Dieu garde, seigneurs, tout le preasse,"[85]
        And of your jangling if ye will cease,
        I will tell you where I have been:
        Sirs, I was at the tavern, and drank wine,
        Methought I saw a piece that was like mine,
        And, sir, all my fingers were arrayed with lime,[86]
        So I conveyed a cup mannerly:
        And yet, i-wis, I played all the fool,
        For there was a scholar of mine own school;[87]
        And, sir, the whoreson espied me.
        Then was I 'rested, and brought in prison;
        For woe then I wist not what to have done,
        And all because I lacked money,
        But a friend in court is worth a penny in purse:
        For Imagination, mine own fellow, i-wis,
        He did help me out full craftily.

---

85. *"Dieu . . . preasse"*] "God keep all here, gentlemen."
86. *lime*] perhaps a reference to bird lime, a sticky substance used to snare birds, but here used to steal a cup.
87. *a scholar . . . school*] i.e., a fellow rascal.

Sirs, he walked through Holborn,
Three hours after the sun was down,
And walked up towards Saint Giles-in-the-Field:
He hoved[88] still, and there beheld,
But there he could not speed of his prey,[89]
And straight to Ludgate he took the way;
Ye wot well, that pothecaries walk[90] very late,
He came to a door and privily spake
To a prentice for a penny-worth of euphorbium,
And also for a halfpenny-worth of alum plumb;
This good servant served him shortly,
And said, Is there ought else that you would buy?
Then he asked for a mouthful of quick brimstone;
And down into the cellar, when the servant was gone,
Aside as he kest[91] his eye,
A great bag of money did he spy,
Therein was an hundred pound:
He trussed him to his feet, and yede[92] his way round,
He was lodged at Newgate at the Swan,
And every man took him for a gentleman;
So on the morrow he delivered me
Out of Newgate by this policy:
And now will I dance and make royal cheer.
But I would Imagination were here,
For he is peerless at need;
Labour to him, sirs, if ye will your matters speed.
Now will I sing, and lustily spring;
But when my fetters on my legs did ring,
I was not glad, perde; but now *Hey, troly, loly.*
Let us see who can descant on this same;
To laugh and get money, it were a good game,
What, whom have we here?
A priest, a doctor, or else a frere.
What, Master Doctor Dotypoll?[93]
Cannot you preach well in a black boll,[94]
Or dispute any divinity?

88. *hoved*] waited, stopped, hovered about.
89. *he . . . prey*] he could not get an opportunity to catch anyone.
90. *walk*] go about their business, work.
91. *kest*] cast.
92. *yede*] went, walked.
93. *Master Doctor Dotypoll*]. Mr. Fool; doty = mentally unbalanced, poll-head.
94. *boll*] bowl.

If ye be cunning, I will put it in a prefe:[95]
Good sir, why do men eat mustard with beef?
By question can you assoil me?
Perseverance.   Peace, man, thou talkest lewdly,
And of thy living, I reed,[96] amend thee.
Freewill.   Avaunt, caitiff, dost thou *thou* me!
I am come of good kin, I tell thee!
My mother was a lady of the stews' blood born,
And (knight of the halter) my father ware an horn;
Therefore I take it in full great scorn,
That thou shouldest thus check me.
Contemplation.   Abide, fellow! thou hast little courtesy,
Thou shalt be charmed, ere thou hence pass,
For thou troubled Pity, and laid on him felony:
Where is Imagination, thy fellow that was?
Freewill.   I defy you both; will you arrest me?
Perseverance.   Nay, nay; thy great words may not help thee,
Fro us thou shalt not escape.
Freewill.   Make room, sirs! that I may break his pate;
I will not be taken for them both.
Contemplation.   Thou shalt abide, whether thou be lief or loth;
Therefore, good son, listen unto me,
And mark these words that I do tell thee:
Thou hast followed thine own will many a day,
And lived in sin without amendment;
Therefore in thy conceit essay
To axe[97] God mercy, and keep His commandment,
Then on thee He will have pity,
And bring thee to heaven that joyful city.
Freewill.   What, whoreson? Will ye have me now a fool?
Nay, yet had I liever be captain of Calais;
For, and I should do after your school,
To learn to patter to make me peevish,
Yet had I liever look with a face full thievish:
And therefore, prate[98] no longer here,
Lest my knave's fist hit you under the ear.
What, ye daws, would ye reed me
For to lese my pleasure in youth and jollity,

95. *prefe*] proof, test.
96. *reed*] counsel, warn, advise.
97. *axe*] ask.
98. *prate*] talk idly, tattle.

To bass[99] and kiss my sweet *trully mully*,
As Jane, Kate, Bess, and Sybil?
I would that hell were full of such prims,
Then would I renne[100] thither on my pins,
As fast as I might go.

Perseverance.   Why, sir, wilt thou not love virtue,
And forsake thy sin for the love of God Almighty?

Freewill.   What God Almighty? by God's fast at Salisbury,
And I trow Easter-day fell on Whitsunday that year,
There were five score save an hundred in my company,
And at petty Judas[101] we made royal cheer,
There had we good ale of Michaelmas brewing;
There heaven-high leaping and springing,
And thus did I
Leap out of Bordeaux unto Canterbury,
Almost ten mile between.

Contemplation.   Freewill, forsake all this world wilfully here,
And change by time; thou oughtest to stand in fear;
For fortune will turn her wheel so swift,
That clean fro thy wealth she will thee lift.

Freewill.   What, lift me, who? and Imagination were here now,
I-wis with his fist he would all-to clout you:
Hence, whoreson, tarry no longer here;
For by Saint Pintle the apostle![102] I swear,
That I will drive you both home,
And yet I was never wont to fight alone:
Alas, that I had not one to bold me,
Then you should see me play the man shamefully;
Alas, it would do me good to fight;
How say you, lords, shall I smite?
Have among you, by this light:
Hence, whoresons, and home at once!
Or with my weapon I shall break your bones.
Avaunt, you knave: walk, by my counsel!

Perseverance.   Son, remember the great pains of hell,
They are so horrible that no tongue can tell;
Beware, lest thou thither do go.

---

99. *bass*] to cuddle, snuggle up to; to give a smacking kiss.
100. *renne*] run.
101. *petty Judas*] unidentified; perhaps a reference to the apostle Judas (not Iscariot).
102. *by . . . apostle!*] a half-humorous, half-obscene oath.

Freewill.   Nay, by Saint Mary! I hope not so;
     I will not go to the devil, while I have my liberty,
     He shall take the labour to fet[103] me, and he will have me;
     For he that will go to hell by his will voluntarily,
     The devil and the whirlwind go with him:
     I will you never fro thence tidings bring;
     Go you before, and show me the way,
     And as to follow you I will not say nay:
     For, by God's body! and you be in once,
     By the mass, I will shit[104] the door at once,
     And then ye be take in a pitfall.
Contemplation.   Now, Jesus, soon defend us from that hole!
     For, "Qui est in inferno nulla est redemptio:"[105]
     Holy Job spake these words full long ago.
Freewill.   Nay, I have done; and you laid out Latin with scope,
     But therewith can you clout[106] me a pair of boots?
     By our lady! ye should have some work of me,
     I would have them well underlaid and easily,
     For I use alway to go on the one side;
     And trow ye how? by God! in the stocks I sat till,
     I trow a three weeks, and more a little stound,[107]
     And there I laboured sore day by day,
     And so I tread my shone[108] inward in good fay;
     Lo, therefore methink you must sole them round.
     If you have any new boots, a pair I would buy,
     But I think your price be too high.
     Sir, once at Newgate I bought a pair of stirrups,
     A mighty pair and a strong,
     A whole year I ware them so long,
     But they came not fully to my knee,
     And to clout them it cost not me a penny:
     Even now, and ye go thither, ye shall find a great heap,
     And you speak in my name, ye shall have good cheap.
Perseverance.   Sir, we came never there, ne never shall do.
Freewill.   Marry! I was taken in a trap there, and tied by the toe,
     That I halted a great while, and might not go.
     I would ye both sat as fast there;

103. *fet*] fetch, carry, bring.
104. *shit*] shut.
105. *"Qui . . . redemptio"*] "For those in hell there is no redemption."
106. *clout*] cobble; make shoes (therewith-with it).
107. *stound*] stunned, amazed, dazed, troubled (by adversity).
108. *shone*] shoon, shoes.

Then should ye dance as a bear,
And all by gangling of your chains.
Contemplation.   Why, sir, were ye there?
Freewill.   Yea, and that is seen by my brains;
　　For, ere I came there, I was as wise as a woodcock,
　　And, I thank God, as witty as a haddock.
　　Yet I trust to recover, as other does,
　　For, and I had once as much wit as a goose,
　　I should be merchant of the bank;
　　Of gold then I should have many a frank,
　　For if I might make three good voyages to Shooter's Hill,
　　And have wind and weather at my will,
　　Then would I never travel the sea more:
　　But it is hard to keep the ship fro the shore,
　　And if it hap to rise a storm,
　　Then thrown in a raft, and so about borne
　　On rocks or brachs for to run,
　　Else to strike aground at Tyburn,
　　That were a mischievous case,
　　For that rock of Tyburn is so perilous a place,
　　Young gallants dare not venture into Kent;
　　But when their money is gone and spent,
　　With their long boots they row on the bay,
　　And any man of war lie by the way,
　　They must take a boat and throw the helm ale;
　　And full hard it is to scape that great jeopardy,
　　For, at Saint Thomas of Watering[109] and they strike a sail,
　　Then must they ride in the haven of hemp without fail;
　　And were not these two jeopardous places indeed,
　　There is many a merchant that thither would speed;
　　But yet we have a sure channel at Westminster,
　　A thousand ships of thieves therein may ride sure;
　　For if they may have anchor-hold and great spending,
　　They may live as merry as any king.
Perseverance.   God wot, sir, there is a piteous living,
　　Then ye dread not the great Master above:
　　Son, forsake thy miss for His love,
　　And then mayst thou come to the bliss also.

---

109. *Saint Thomas of Watering*] a place of execution located at the second milestone on the
　　road from London to Canterbury. Here there was a brook (for *watering* horses); the
　　place was named for St. Thomas à Becket since it was located on the road to his shrine
　　at Canterbury.

Freewill.   Why, what would you that I should do?
Contemplation.   For to go toward heaven.
Freewill.   Marry! and you will me thither bring,
     I would do after you.
Perserverance.   I pray you, remember my words now:
     Freewill, bethink thee that thou shalt die,
     And of the hour thou are uncertain,
     Yet by thy life thou mayest find a remedy;
     For, and thou die in sin, all labour is in vain,
     Then shall thy soul be still in pain.
     Lost and damned for evermore;
     Help is past, though thou would fain,
     Then thou wilt curse the time that thou were bore.
Freewill.   Sir, if ye will undertake that I saved shall be,
     I will do all the penance that you will set me.
Contemplation.   If that thou for thy sins be sorry,
     Our Lord will forgive thee them.
Freewill.   Now of all my sins I axe God mercy;
     Here I forsake sin, and trust to amend:
     I beseech Jesu that is most mighty
     To forgive all that I have offend.
Perseverance.   Our Lord now will show thee His mercy,
     A new name thou need none have;
     For all that will to heaven high,
     By his own freewill he must forsake folly,
     Then is he sure and safe.
Contemplation.   Hold here a new garment,
     And hereafter live devoutly,
     And for thy sins do ever repent:
     Sorrow for thy sins is very remedy:
     And, Freewill, ever to virtue apply,
     Also to sadness give ye attendance,
     Let him never out of remembrance.
Freewill.   I will never from you, sir Perseverance;
     With you will I abide both day and night,
     Of mind never to be variable,
     And God's commandments to keep them right,
     In deed and word, and ever full stable.
Perseverance.   Then heaven thou shalt have without fable,[110]
     But look that thou be steadfast,
     And let thy mind with good will last.

110. *fable*] an untruth, a falsehood.

[*Enter Imagination.*]

Imagination.   Huff, huff, huff! who sent after me?
    I am Imagination, full of jollity,
    Lord, that my heart is light,
    When shall I perish? I trow, never;
    By Christ! I reck[111] not a feather:
    Even now I was dubbed a knight,
    Where at Tyburn of the collar,
    And of the stews I am made controller —
    Of all the houses of lechery;
    There shall no man play doccy[112] there,
    At the Bell, Hartshorn, ne elsewhere,
    Without they have leave of me.
    But, sirs, wot ye why I am come hither?
    By our lady! to gather good company together:
    Saw ye not of my fellow Freewill?
    I am afraid lest he be searching on a hill;
    By God! then one of us is beguiled.
    What fellow is this that in this coat is filed?
    Cock's death! whom have we here?
    What, Freewill, mine own fere?
    Art thou out of thy mind?
Freewill.   God grant the way to heaven that I may find;
    For I forsake thy company.
Imagination.   God's arms! my company? and why?
Freewill.   For thou livest too sinfully.
Imagination.   Alas! tell me how it is with thee.
Freewill.   Forsake thy sin for the love of me.
Imagination.   Cock's heart! art thou waxed mad?
Freewill.   When I think on my sin, it makes me full sad.
Imagination.   God's wounds! who gave thee that counsel?
Freewill.   Perseverance and Contemplation, I thee tell.
Imagination.   A vengeance on them, I would they were in hell!
Freewill.   Amend, Imagination, and mercy cry!
Imagination.   By God's sides! I had liever be hanged on high;
    Nay, that would I not do: I had liever die.
    By God's passion! and I had a long knife,
    I would bereave these two whoresons of their life:
    How, how? twenty pounds for a dagger!

111. *reck*] care for, mind.
112. *doccy*] "duxy" generally meant a loose woman, but the term was also used of men; to
    "play doxy" meant to whore.

Contemplation.   Peace, peace, good son, and speak softer,
    And amend, ere death draw his draught;
    For on thee he will steal full soft,
    He giveth never no man warning,
    And ever to thee he is coming:
    Therefore remember thee well.
Imagination.   Ah, whoreson! if I were jailer of hell,
    I-wis, some sorrow should thou feel;
    For to the devil I would thee sell,
    Then should ye have many a sorry meal,
    I would never give you meat ne drink,
    Ye should fast, whoresons, till ye did stink,
    Even as a rotten dog; yea, by Saint Tyburn of Kent!
Perseverance.   Imagination, think what God did for thee;
    On Good Friday He hanged on a tree,
    And spent all His precious blood,
    A spear did rive[113] His heart asunder,
    The gates He brake up with a clap of thunder,
    And Adam and Eve there delivered He.
Imagination.   What devil! what is that to me?
    By God's fast! I was ten year in Newgate,
    And many more fellows with me sat,
    Yet he never came there to help me ne my company.
Contemplation.   Yes, he holp thee, or thou haddest not been here now.
Imagination.   By the mass, I cannot show you,
    For he and I never drank together,
    Yet I know many an ale stake;[114]
    Neither at the stews, i-wis, he never came thither:
    Goeth he arrayed in white or in black?
    For, and he out of prison had holp me,
    I know well once I should him see.
    What gown weareth he, I pray you?
Perseverance.   Sir, he halp you out by his might.
Imagination.   I cannot tell you, by this light;
    But methought that I lay there too long,
    And the whoreson fetters were so strong,
    That had almost brought my neck out of joint.
Perseverance.   Amend, son, and thou shalt know him,
    That delivered thee out of prison;

---

113. *rive*] split, tear.
114. *ale stake*] a stake or pole, usually decorated with a garland, used as the sign of an
    alehouse; the term was also used, as here, to denote a tippler.

And if thou wilt forsake thy miss,
Surely thou shalt come to the bliss,
And be inheritor of heaven.
Imagination.   What, sir, above the moon?
Nay, by the mass, then should I fall soon;
Yet I keep not to climb so high;
But to climb for a bird's nest,
There is none between east and west,
That dare thereto venter[115] better than I:
But to venter to heaven — what, and my feet slip?
I know well then I should break my neck,
And, by God, then had I the worse side;
Yet had I liever be by the nose tied
In a wench's arse somewhere,
Rather than I would stand in that great fear,
For to go up to heaven — nay, I pray you, let be.
Freewill.   Imagination, wilt thou do by the counsel of me?
Imagination.   Yea, sir, by my troth, whatsomever it be.
Freewill.   Amend yet for my sake,
It is better betime than too late;
How say you? will you God's hests[116] fulfil?
Imagination.   I will do, sir, even as you will;
But, I pray you, let me have a new coat,
When I have need, and in my purse a groat,
Then will I dwell with you still.
Freewill.   Beware! for when thou art buried in the ground,
Few friends for thee will be found,
Remember this still!
Imagination.   No thing dread I so sore as death,
Therefore to amend I think it be time;
Sin have I used all the days of my breath,
With pleasure, lechery, and misusing,
And spent amiss my five wits; therefore I am sorry.
Here of all my sins I axe God mercy.
Perseverance.   Hold! here is a better clothing for thee,
And look that thou forsake thy folly;
Be steadfast, look that thou fall never.
Imagination.   Now here I forsake my sin for ever.
Freewill.   Sir, wait thou now on Perseverance,
For thy name shall be called Good Remembrance;

115. *venter*] venture.
116. *hests*] behests; injunctions, commands, orders.

And I will dwell with Contemplation,
And follow him wherever he become.
Contemplation.   Well, are ye so both agreed?
Imagination.   Yea, sir, so God me speed.
Perseverance.   Sir, ye shall wait on me soon,
And be God's servant day and night,
And in every place where ye become,
Give good counsel to every wight:
And men axe your name, tell you Remembrance,
That God's law keepeth truly every day;
And look that ye forget not repentance,
Then to heaven ye shall go the next way,
Where ye shall see in the heavenly quere[117]
The blessed company of saints so holy,
That lived devoutly while they were here:
Unto the which bliss I beseech God Almighty
To bring there your souls that here be present,
And unto virtuous living that ye may apply,
Truly for to keep His commandments;
Of all our mirths here we make an end,
Unto the bliss of heaven Jesus your souls bring.

AMEN.

117. *quere*] choir.

DOVER·THRIFT·EDITIONS

PLAYS

LIFE IS A DREAM, Pedro Calderón de la Barca. 96pp. 0-486-42124-4

H. M. S. PINAFORE, William Schwenck Gilbert. 64pp. 0-486-41114-1

THE MIKADO, William Schwenck Gilbert. 64pp. 0-486-27268-0

SHE STOOPS TO CONQUER, Oliver Goldsmith. 80pp. 0-486-26867-5

THE LOWER DEPTHS, Maxim Gorky. 80pp. 0-486-41115-X

A DOLL'S HOUSE, Henrik Ibsen. 80pp. 0-486-27062-9

GHOSTS, Henrik Ibsen. 64pp. 0-486-29852-3

HEDDA GABLER, Henrik Ibsen. 80pp. 0-486-26469-6

PEER GYNT, Henrik Ibsen. 144pp. 0-486-42686-6

THE WILD DUCK, Henrik Ibsen. 96pp. 0-486-41116-8

VOLPONE, Ben Jonson. 112pp. 0-486-28049-7

DR. FAUSTUS, Christopher Marlowe. 64pp. 0-486-28208-2

TAMBURLAINE, Christopher Marlowe. 128pp. 0-486-42125-2

THE IMAGINARY INVALID, Molière. 96pp. 0-486-43789-2

THE MISANTHROPE, Molière. 64pp. 0-486-27065-3

RIGHT YOU ARE, IF YOU THINK YOU ARE, Luigi Pirandello. 64pp. (Not available in Europe or United Kingdom.) 0-486-29576-1

SIX CHARACTERS IN SEARCH OF AN AUTHOR, Luigi Pirandello. 64pp. (Not available in Europe or United Kingdom.) 0-486-29992-9

PHÈDRE, Jean Racine. 64pp. 0-486-41927-4

HANDS AROUND, Arthur Schnitzler. 64pp. 0-486-28724-6

ANTONY AND CLEOPATRA, William Shakespeare. 128pp. 0-486-40062-X

AS YOU LIKE IT, William Shakespeare. 80pp. 0-486-40432-3

HAMLET, William Shakespeare. 128pp. 0-486-27278-8

HENRY IV, William Shakespeare. 96pp. 0-486-29584-2

JULIUS CAESAR, William Shakespeare. 80pp. 0-486-26876-4

KING LEAR, William Shakespeare. 112pp. 0-486-28058-6

LOVE'S LABOUR'S LOST, William Shakespeare. 64pp. 0-486-41929-0

MACBETH, William Shakespeare. 96pp. 0-486-27802-6

MEASURE FOR MEASURE, William Shakespeare. 96pp. 0-486-40889-2

THE MERCHANT OF VENICE, William Shakespeare. 96pp. 0-486-28492-1

A MIDSUMMER NIGHT'S DREAM, William Shakespeare. 80pp. 0-486-27067-X

MUCH ADO ABOUT NOTHING, William Shakespeare. 80pp. 0-486-28272-4

OTHELLO, William Shakespeare. 112pp. 0-486-29097-2

RICHARD III, William Shakespeare. 112pp. 0-486-28747-5

ROMEO AND JULIET, William Shakespeare. 96pp. 0-486-27557-4

THE TAMING OF THE SHREW, William Shakespeare. 96pp. 0-486-29765-9

THE TEMPEST, William Shakespeare. 96pp. 0-486-40658-X

TWELFTH NIGHT; OR, WHAT YOU WILL, William Shakespeare. 80pp. 0-486-29290-8

ARMS AND THE MAN, George Bernard Shaw. 80pp. (Not available in Europe or United Kingdom.) 0-486-26476-9

HEARTBREAK HOUSE, George Bernard Shaw. 128pp. (Not available in Europe or United Kingdom.) 0-486-29291-6

PYGMALION, George Bernard Shaw. 96pp. (Available in U.S. only.) 0-486-28222-8

THE RIVALS, Richard Brinsley Sheridan. 96pp. 0-486-40433-1

THE SCHOOL FOR SCANDAL, Richard Brinsley Sheridan. 96pp. 0-486-26687-7

ANTIGONE, Sophocles. 64pp. 0-486-27804-2

OEDIPUS AT COLONUS, Sophocles. 64pp. 0-486-40659-8

OEDIPUS REX, Sophocles. 64pp. 0-486-26877-2

DOVER · THRIFT · EDITIONS

PLAYS

ELECTRA, Sophocles. 64pp. 0-486-28482-4

MISS JULIE, August Strindberg. 64pp. 0-486-27281-8

THE PLAYBOY OF THE WESTERN WORLD AND RIDERS TO THE SEA, J. M. Synge. 80pp. 0-486-27562-0

THE DUCHESS OF MALFI, John Webster. 96pp. 0-486-40660-1

THE IMPORTANCE OF BEING EARNEST, Oscar Wilde. 64pp. 0-486-26478-5

LADY WINDERMERE'S FAN, Oscar Wilde. 64pp. 0-486-40078-6

BOXED SETS

FAVORITE JANE AUSTEN NOVELS: *Pride and Prejudice, Sense and Sensibility* and *Persuasion* (Complete and Unabridged), Jane Austen. 800pp. 0-486-29748-9

BEST WORKS OF MARK TWAIN: Four Books, Dover. 624pp. 0-486-40226-6

EIGHT GREAT GREEK TRAGEDIES: Six Books, Dover. 480pp. 0-486-40203-7

FIVE GREAT ENGLISH ROMANTIC POETS, Dover. 496pp. 0-486-27893-X

GREAT AFRICAN-AMERICAN WRITERS: Seven Books, Dover. 704pp. 0-486-29995-3

GREAT WOMEN POETS: 4 Complete Books, Dover. 256pp. (Available in U.S. only.) 0-486-28388-7

MASTERPIECES OF RUSSIAN LITERATURE: Seven Books, Dover. 880pp. 0-486-40665-2

SIX GREAT AMERICAN POETS: Poems by Poe, Dickinson, Whitman, Longfellow, Frost, and Millay, Dover. 512pp. (Available in U.S. only.) 0-486-27425-X

FAVORITE NOVELS AND STORIES: Four Complete Books, Jack London. 568pp. 0-486-42216-X

FIVE GREAT SCIENCE FICTION NOVELS, H. G. Wells. 640pp. 0-486-43978-X

FIVE GREAT PLAYS OF SHAKESPEARE, Dover. 496pp. 0-486-27892-1

TWELVE PLAYS BY SHAKESPEARE, William Shakespeare. 1,173pp. 0-486-44336-1

All books complete and unabridged. All 5³⁄₁₆" x 8¼", paperbound. Available at your book dealer, online at **www.doverpublications.com**, or by writing to Dept. GI, Dover Publications, Inc., 31 East 2nd Street, Mineola, NY 11501. For current price information or for free catalogs (please indicate field of interest), write to Dover Publications or log on to **www.doverpublications.com** and see every Dover book in print. Dover publishes more than 500 books each year on science, elementary and advanced mathematics, biology, music, art, literary history, social sciences, and other areas.